SOMETHIN

He still doesn't get i̶... e doesn't understand how I could voluntarily leave him behind for two months. But if he doesn't understand why I went to California, how will he ever be able to really understand me?

Realizing that Alex was waiting for her to speak, Lisa forced herself to smile as if nothing were wrong. *Nothing is wrong, she told herself firmly. Even the best couples don't necessarily have to share every single thought and feeling they have. The most important thing right now is to reassure Alex—make him realize how important he is to me. And if that means not talking about California with him, so be it. It's not that big a deal. I'm sure we'll be able to discuss it someday, after we've both had some time to readjust. Nothing has changed.*

But deep in her heart, Lisa couldn't help thinking that for the first time since they'd fallen in love, something *had* changed between them. And she wasn't quite sure how to fix it.

**Don't miss any of the excitement
at Pine Hollow,
where friends come first:**

PINE HOLLOW™

CHANGING LEADS

BY BONNIE BRYANT

BANTAM BOOKS
NEW YORK • TORONTO • LONDON • SYDNEY • AUCKLAND

Special thanks to Sir "B" Farms and Laura and Vinny Marino

RL 5.0, ages 12 and up

CHANGING LEADS
A Bantam Book / February 1999

"Pine Hollow" is a trademark of Bonnie Bryant Hiller.

ISBN 0-553-49245-4

Published simultaneously in the United States and Canada

Bantam Books are published by Bantam Books, a division of Random House,
Inc. Its trademark, consisting of the words "Bantam Books" and the portrayal
of a rooster, is Registered in U.S. Patent and Trademark Office and in other
countries. Marca Registrada. Bantam Books, 1540 Broadway, New York, New
York 10036.

PRINTED IN THE UNITED STATES OF AMERICA

OPM   0 9 8 7 6 5 4 3 2 1

My special thanks to Catherine Hapka for her help in the writing of this book.

ONE

"Callie! Yo, Callie!" Stevie Lake called over the shouts and laughter echoing off the walls of the crowded school hallway. Callie Forester was a few yards ahead of her, leaning over the water fountain near the north stairwell. "Callie!"

Callie turned and waited for Stevie to dodge through the throng of other students. "No problem there," she joked wryly. "I think a turtle could catch up to me these days if it really tried."

Stevie winced as she glanced at Callie's ugly metal crutches. Callie was leaning on them heavily, taking the weight off her right leg. "Sorry about that," Stevie muttered. "I didn't mean to say anything to—"

Callie waved away the apology. "Stop it," she ordered. "It was a joke. You know—ha ha, funny?"

Stevie grinned weakly. "Ha ha," she said. "Funny."

Stevie was famous for her quick sense of humor,

1

but she couldn't find much to laugh about when it came to Callie's condition. The girl had residual brain damage that had forced her to learn how to use the right side of her body all over again. Stevie had been driving on that stormy afternoon a little more than two months before, so it was only natural that she would retain some guilt about what had happened, no matter how many times other people—including Callie—reminded her that the accident hadn't been her fault. Stevie knew by now that she couldn't have prevented her car from flipping over on the rain-slick road in front of Pine Hollow Stables any more than she could have prevented the sun from rising that morning. But knowing it in her head wasn't the same as believing it deep in her heart.

So while Callie had spent a lot of time and energy in the months since the accident working to overcome her physical problems, Stevie had struggled just as hard to come to terms with her mental and emotional ones, and things were a lot better now for both of them. Still, Callie was starting the new year at a new school with crutches and a pronounced limp and Stevie sometimes had trouble watching her new friend trying to walk or stand up or mount a horse or do any of the other simple little things that most people took for granted.

Stevie willed herself to focus on Callie's face

rather than her weakened right leg. "Anyway, how are you surviving your first day at dear old Fenton Hall?" She waved a hand to indicate the chaos of bustling, shouting, laughing students that buzzed around them. "I've barely seen you all day."

"I know." Callie's dark blue eyes wandered from Stevie's face to take in the noisy scene. "I was hoping I'd have some classes with you. It would make it a lot easier if I had a friend to sit with on the first day instead of just sort of hovering awkwardly until everyone else is sitting down."

Stevie nodded sympathetically. She knew that Callie could seem a bit arrogant and intimidating at first meeting—to some people at least. The fact that she was a congressman's daughter probably had something to do with putting people off, although Stevie was sure that Callie's natural reserve and steely, sometimes overserious determination had even more to do with it. Stevie herself had warmed up to Callie right away; but then again, Stevie wasn't always sensitive to such subtleties. She tended to like everyone she met until someone gave her a reason not to, and so far Callie hadn't given her any such reason. Over the past couple of months, Stevie had come to think of Callie as a close friend, and she had soon recognized that the new girl's cool exterior hid a person who was actually quite shy and uncertain in a lot of ways—the

3

kind of person who would hesitate to sit down in a classroom full of strangers until the last possible moment. "At least you know a few other people," Stevie said encouragingly. "You know, like some of the other riders from Pine Hollow. Right?"

"True," Callie agreed. "Lorraine Olsen is in my history class, and that cute little guy with the dimples—George, is it?—is in my chemistry class." She rolled her eyes. "It's a good thing, too. I'm going to need a study buddy in that one. It's only the first day, and I'm already confused."

"Uh-oh," Stevie joked. "If you're confused, I'm sure to be totally lost. I have chem next period. Maybe I'll come down with a sudden stomachache in the next"—she glanced at her watch—"four and a half minutes."

Callie raised one eyebrow, looking bemused. "That might work for today," she said. "But what about the rest of the year?"

Stevie shrugged. "Hey, what can I say? I think it's a new virus. It recurs every day right around sixth period."

Callie laughed, and Stevie chuckled along. It was nice to have a new friend to chat with in the halls, even if they didn't have many classes together. Unlike Callie, Stevie wasn't the least bit shy, and she never let anything stop her from getting to know people. She had dozens of casual friends and hundreds of acquaintances at school, from her fellow members of the Fenton Hall student council to the ever-shifting group of people who sat at her favorite lunch table at the far end of the cafeteria. But her closest friends had always been at Pine Hollow Stables. She had met Carole Hanson and Lisa Atwood there when they were all in junior high school, and the three girls had been inseparable ever since. Carole and Lisa both attended Willow Creek High School on the other side of town, which meant that Stevie didn't get to spend nearly as much time with them as she would have liked, especially with family, homework, boyfriends, jobs, and other activities taking up so much of all their free time.

Callie shifted her weight slightly, resting an elbow against the water fountain behind her. "I guess I should look on the bright side," she said. "At least I'm the right age to be taking chemistry. Back home it was a senior class, so Scott hasn't taken it yet." Her eyes twinkled. "Believe me, he's not thrilled about getting stuck in a class full of us lowly juniors."

This time Stevie's laugh came a little less easily as she thought about Callie's brother. Scott Forester was a friendly, outgoing, eminently likable guy, a star of his hometown debate team and a surefire candidate to follow in his father's political footsteps. Unlike the more withdrawn Callie, he seemed able to get along effortlessly with almost everyone he met—but not with Stevie. Not anymore. Scott still blamed Stevie for the accident and his sister's condition, even though Callie and her parents had long since forgiven her and the police had cleared her of any blame. Scott couldn't quite seem to forgive and forget; he didn't talk to Stevie in the easy way he once had. He couldn't even meet her eye when they passed in the aisle at the stables.

Stevie tore her thoughts away from Callie's brother and turned them back to Callie. "What class do you have now?"

Callie pulled her schedule out of her pocket and squinted at it. "Latin," she reported. "Ugh. That was my worst class back home. I didn't want to take it this year, but my dad insisted." She grimaced. "He said it was because 'Foresters aren't quitters,' but I think he's really just trying to torture me— and keep me out of trouble and the media spotlight."

Stevie grinned. Congressman Forester was sensitive about publicity issues, but Stevie could tell Callie was just kidding around. "Oh, well," she said. "I've been taking Latin for two years and all I remember is that *equus* means 'horse.' Still, who said school was supposed to be fun? At least we have our picnic to look forward to this weekend."

She sighed with anticipation as she thought about

that, wishing it were Saturday already. Stevie, Carole, and Lisa had come up with the idea for the picnic the afternoon before as they were cleaning tack after their traditional last-day-of-summer-before-school-opens trail ride. Stevie had been bemoaning the start of yet another school year, claiming that she wasn't sure she would be able to survive all those hours of dull lectures and duller homework. Carole had been quick to agree, obviously thinking that every minute spent at school was a minute spent away from the stable. Even Lisa, who was an excellent student and actually liked school most of the time, had admitted that she wasn't quite prepared for the summer to end, especially since she had just returned to Willow Creek from a two-month stay with her father in California.

"It's always kind of sad when summer ends," Carole had said, sounding wistful as she scrubbed slowly at her horse's bridle. "Things always get so busy at the beginning of the school year, don't they? There never seems to be enough time for the important stuff."

Stevie had opened her mouth to argue. They had all stayed plenty busy that summer, school or no school. Carole had spent practically every waking hour at Pine Hollow, working hard at her job as morning stable manager, while Stevie had spent far too many hours counting change and handing out detergent at her summer job at a local laundry. But Stevie shrugged and admitted, "I know what you mean. Time seems different in the summer. The days are longer, there's more time for hanging out—"

"Going on trail rides," Lisa put in.

Carole sighed. "Swimming and talking and spending time with friends."

The idea for the picnic had seemed to come to all of them at once, like many of their best ideas. After that, all that was left was to plan it—and decide what to call it. Stevie was torn between calling it a last blast of summer or an I-survived-my-first-week-of-school party. Either way, the girls had quickly decided to make a real celebration of it by inviting a few close friends: Phil Marsten, Stevie's longtime boyfriend, who lived in the next county; Phil's best friend, A. J. McDonnell; A.J.'s girlfriend, Julianna; Stevie's twin brother, Alex, who also happened to be Lisa's boyfriend; and Callie, of course.

"You're still coming, aren't you?" Stevie asked Callie now. "Latin homework or no Latin homework?"

Callie's expression brightened. "Definitely," she said. "I wouldn't miss it." She shot Stevie an unreadable glance. "Scott still says he can't make it. But I'll see what I can do to change his mind."

Stevie nodded, keeping her expression as neutral as she could. When Stevie had called the night before to invite Callie, she had also made a point of inviting Callie's brother. But Scott had immediately declined, and Stevie was sure it was because of her.

"Anyway," Callie went on, seeming to sense Stevie's discomfort, "I'm sure we'll have plenty of fun without him. Now that my leg is getting strong enough, I'm looking forward to testing it on a nice long trail ride."

"Good." Stevie glanced at her watch again. "Oops. I'd better run. My chem class is upstairs, and I'd hate to be late on my first day."

"See you." Callie smiled, then straightened her crutches and started down the hallway with her awkward, uneven stride.

Stevie watched her for a moment, then turned away, fighting back twinges of guilt. *It's amazing she's made this much progress this fast,* she reminded herself, trying to look on the bright side. *Her doctors keep saying they've never seen anything quite like it.* She smiled. *Then again, they probably never met anyone quite like Callie before.*

As she hurried toward the broad marble staircase at the center of the hall, her thoughts returned to Scott. Part of her was relieved that he wouldn't be coming along on Saturday. It would make things a lot more comfortable, meaning that she would be free to enjoy her friends' company without worrying about what Scott was thinking. But another part of her was disappointed. As long as Scott continued to hate her, Stevie wasn't sure she would ever be able to return to her old, happy-go-lucky, preaccident self. And the longer he ignored her, the less likely it seemed that things could ever go back to normal between them. Stevie was smart and experienced enough to know that sometimes things really didn't work out for the best, that some people just couldn't get along no matter how hard they tried. But that wouldn't be true of her and Scott, could it? It didn't seem possible. They were both friendly, intelligent, rational people—in most ways, anyway. If he would just give her a chance, spend some time with her, try to get over his anger instead of ignoring her . . .

Still, if he doesn't want to come on Saturday, he doesn't have to, Stevie told herself as she walked into her chemistry classroom. *And just because he actually nodded to me when I saw him at Pine Hollow yesterday doesn't mean he's suddenly ready to be my best friend. What is it that Mom always tells me? Two steps forward, one step back.*

She did her best to push those thoughts out of her mind. She was going to need to focus her attention on this class if she had any hope of doing well. As she headed for an empty desk near the door, she glanced over the students already seated—and spotted a very familiar face in the front row. It was Scott.

Stevie gulped, suddenly remembering what Callie had said about her brother's taking chemistry this year. As she stared, Scott looked up and saw her. His eyes met hers for the briefest of moments, registering surprise. Then his expression went blank, and he coolly turned away.

Stevie rolled her eyes and dropped her books on the scarred wooden desk with a thump. *Great,* she thought. *This is just what I need.*

At that very moment Carole Hanson was pinching herself on the arm, trying desperately to stay awake. She was sitting in the last row of her algebra class, bored out of her mind.

When am I ever going to need to know even the slightest little thing about this stuff, anyway? she thought, feeling disgruntled. *I didn't even want to take Algebra I freshman year. Now here I am, stuck learning even more boring, useless, totally incomprehensible garbage in Algebra II.*

She glanced at the portly, balding man standing at the front of the room. Mr. Whiteside seemed to be taking whatever it was he was currently babbling about—integers or something—really seriously. For that matter, so did the other students. Most of them were scribbling notes as if their lives depended on it. But Carole couldn't quite manage to share their feeling of urgency.

Why do all my teachers feel the need to plunge right into the thick of things? Carole wondered idly. *Why can't they just give us a few days—or weeks—to recover from summer vacation and get used to being trapped here again?*

But Carole knew that even if the teachers gave her six months, she would still have trouble adjusting to being stuck in class. For most of her life she had been a dutiful student. She had done her homework, kept up with her assignments, and not thought much about school one way or the other. But last year that had started to change. She had begun to wonder exactly why she had to spend all these hours studying subjects she didn't care about and would never need to know. She had known for most of her life that she would work with horses someday. Now "someday" was getting close enough to taste, and she was starting to resent anything— math class, history class, English class—that stood in the way of learning everything she could about horses. Over the summer it had been easy enough to ignore such thoughts, since her job at Pine Hollow had kept her busy and happy. But now . . . It was only the first day of school, and Carole was already as restless as a horse that had been cooped up in a straight stall too long.

The only thing that kept her from complete despair was the thought that high school was the last step to college and a major in equine studies. The year before, thinking about all the useful things she would learn after high school had made it possible for her to sit through her classes day after day, listening to teachers spout off about all kinds of useless stuff. She just hoped those thoughts would be enough to carry her through this year . . . and next . . .

Carole felt her head falling forward heavily, and she quickly blinked and sat upright. She reminded herself that there was another reason she couldn't afford to ignore her teachers. Max Regnery, the owner of Pine Hollow, had a strict rule about grades. Any student who rode at his stable had to keep a C average or higher in all classes or he cut off the student's riding privileges. He was as serious about that particular rule now that Carole was a high-school junior as he had been back when she was in junior high.

Thinking of Max's rule made Carole think of Max himself. The day before, as she was cooling down Starlight after the end-of-summer trail ride with her friends, Max had called her aside, saying he wanted to talk to her. Carole had assumed that he merely wanted to discuss the changes in her duties around Pine Hollow now that school was starting. He had wanted to talk about that, but first he'd had some other news to share with her. Some surprising, thrilling, worrisome, exciting, terrifying, and complicated news.

I still can't believe it, she thought, automatically crossing her second and third fingers for luck as she had done since she was a little girl riding toward a tough fence. She had crossed them that way so as not to jeopardize her grip on the reins, and it had become a habit. *I can't believe I didn't have a clue about this before. And I can't believe he actually expects me to keep it a secret. How can I not tell my best friends something so wonderful?*

Still, she knew there were at least a couple of reasons why Max didn't want anyone else to know about this yet. Good, practical reasons. Besides, he was her boss, and he had given her a direct order. Carole had spent long enough as the daughter of a Marine colonel to know what that meant. She had to keep her mouth shut, like it or not. Even if it did make her feel as if she was being a disloyal friend. Even if it had been next to impossible to hide her thoughts from Lisa and Stevie as they all chatted in the tack room a few minutes later. Even if every fiber in her being had wanted to break down and shout with excitement and then spill the beans . . .

She shook her head again briskly, as if by doing so she could shake those thoughts from her mind. Max didn't want her to tell anyone yet. That was all there was to it. Daydreaming about how her friends would react to the news—which they would hear soon enough anyhow if all went well—was almost as much of a waste of time as learning algebra.

Her deep brown eyes wandered toward the wide windows at one side of the room as, with a concerted effort, she turned her thoughts to more neutral topics. It was a beautiful late-summer day, and the weather promised to hold through evening at least. Carole was happy about that. She planned to head over to Pine Hollow right after school to give Starlight a good workout over some jumps in the outdoor schooling ring. Starlight had been fairly young when Carole's father had bought him for her for Christmas a few years earlier, and Carole had been training him ever since, honing his technique and increasing his skills. The bay gelding was a talented jumper, and she had enjoyed molding him into the calm, confident, accomplished horse he was today. Together they had entered a number of shows and won quite a few ribbons.

Speaking of shows, Carole thought, *it would be so cool if Starlight and I could enter the Colesford Horse Show. Now* that *would be a real test of his ability. Mine too.*

She sighed and doodled absently in the margins of her math book as she thought about the article she'd read a few days earlier in the latest issue of her favorite horse magazine. The nearby town of Colesford had never hosted a major horse show before, but it was debuting with style. The article had raved for several pages about all the fabulous horses and famous riders already signed up to compete.

For a second, Carole allowed herself to sink into a daydream. . . . *Starlight and I will be the underdogs, of course. When we ride into the ring for the stadium jumping event, hardly anyone will even applaud. But the second Starlight clears the first jump, the spectators will start to take notice. Then, by halfway through our clean round, they'll realize that we are moving faster than any other competitor so far. Then . . .*

She forced herself to snap out of it. Carole loved her horse, but she was realistic about him, too. When she was younger, she had been quite sure that her beautiful bay gelding could jump the moon if she asked him to. But now, with a little more experience under her belt, Carole knew that while Starlight was good, he wasn't in the same league as the horses that would be jumping at Colesford. Not now, and probably not ever. It would be a waste of time and effort to enter the prestigious show—not to mention a tremendous waste of money. There was no way Carole could afford the entry fees, which according to the article were exorbitant even by horse show standards. Most of what she earned working part-time at Pine Hollow went toward Starlight's care. And she didn't want to ask her father for money, not for this show. It wasn't that Colonel Hanson couldn't or wouldn't pay if she asked. And it wasn't that Carole didn't think there were valuable lessons to be learned at every show. But with so little chance of winning, she had to admit—reluctantly—that it just didn't seem worth the money.

Finding these thoughts a bit depressing, Carole once again forced herself to change tracks and think of something else. Something more pleasant. Like the latter part of her discussion with Max the afternoon before—the part when they had talked about her new duties at Pine Hollow.

"I know you've had to deal with a lot of the paperwork and grunt work this summer, Carole," Max had said rather apologetically.

"It's okay," she had assured him quickly. "It's all part of running a stable, right? That means it's automatically interesting."

Max had cocked a skeptical eyebrow.

Carole had grinned weakly. "Well, okay," she'd amended. "Maybe 'interesting' isn't the right way to describe it. How about 'an unfortunate part of the job'?"

"Okay, I'll buy that." Max had chuckled. "In any case, now that Denise has started as full-time stable manager and you're going to be back at school, I think it's time to shift things around a bit."

"What do you mean?" Carole had been a little wary. The last time Max had talked about shifting things around, a couple of years before, he had ended up selling half a dozen Pine Hollow school horses to a stable in the next state, including a few of Carole's old favorites like Coconut and Tecumseh. That had been a shift, all right. Carole wasn't sure she was ready for another big change like that.

But Max was smiling. "I mean, part of the reason you're working here is to learn everything about running a stable, right?" He waited for her to nod, then continued. "Well, there's more to it than paperwork, although sometimes it doesn't feel like it. I think it's time to give you a taste of some of the more interesting aspects of stable work before you decide to chuck it all and become an accountant or a stockbroker or something."

Carole had grinned, knowing that he was kidding.

Now, as she thought back on the conversation, the possibilities of what those new tasks might include made Carole shiver with anticipation. But her job wasn't the only thing she was looking forward to. She also couldn't wait until Saturday and the big barbecue blowout by the banks of Willow Creek. It would be the perfect way to celebrate the end of the first week of school. Besides, she was looking forward to hanging out with her friends. Lisa had spent most of the summer in California, and Carole herself had put in an awful lot of hours at the stable. It would be nice to just kick back, relax, enjoy each other and the day and the horses. . . . Plus she would get to see A.J. for the first time in a while, and his girlfriend, too. . . . Callie would be able to show off the progress she'd been making in her physical therapy. . . .

Carole felt herself drifting off again. Mr. Whiteside's voice was just a little too deep and soothing—it was putting her straight to sleep.

She forced herself to sit up straighter. That worked for a few seconds. But when she tried to focus on what the teacher was saying, she felt herself slumping again, against her will, deeper into her seat.

She pinched herself on the arm again—harder this time. Too hard.

"Ouch!" she cried involuntarily.

Mr. Whiteside paused and peered at her over the tops of his rimless glasses, looking surprised. "Ms.—

er—Hanson?" he said, after glancing at his seating chart. "Did you have something to add?"

Carole felt her face turning bright red. "No, sir," she muttered. "Sorry."

As the teacher turned back to the chalkboard to continue his lecture, Carole slumped down into her seat again. But this time she wasn't the least bit sleepy.

I'm not sure I can take two more whole years of this! she thought desperately.

Lisa Atwood was only a few doors down from Carole, but her thoughts were miles away—in California, to be exact. *Maybe I should have stayed out there and lived with Dad after all,* she thought, only half jokingly. *Then maybe I'd be learning something right now instead of sitting here feeling my brain cells rot from underuse.* She was annoyed because her calculus teacher seemed to think that the students were so brain-dead from their summer vacations that he should just let them laze around for the first few days of school instead of getting down to work.

She glanced toward the front of the room, where her teacher, a thin-lipped young man named Mr. Halliday, was pontificating about his five favorite action movies of the past summer. The other students seemed to be enjoying the exercise, calling out their own opinions and cracking jokes.

But Lisa found her mind wandering. She wasn't really surprised—she had no interest in action movies. But then again, she had found herself having trouble focusing even in the few classes where her teachers had actually started teaching. She guessed she was still adjusting to being home after a summer away.

Most of the time her homecoming felt exactly the way it should—like a return to the people and places and routines she knew and loved, where everything made sense and moved along as it always had. Her trail ride the day before with Carole and Stevie was a perfect example. As they had ridden along the familiar trails behind Pine Hollow, she could almost have closed her eyes and imagined that they were all still as young and carefree as they'd been back in junior high when the three of them had started The Saddle Club and talked about nothing but horses all day long. Then there was Alex. Her reunion with him had been even more wonderful than she had expected. Somehow, being apart had made their bond—and their attraction—stronger than ever. After just a few days back together, Lisa couldn't imagine how she had ever survived two long months without him. In fact, the two of them had slid so easily back into their relationship that it already felt almost as if the summer separation had never happened.

Still, at other times she found herself taken by surprise at the amount of adjusting she had to do. For one thing, spending two months in a loving, happy home with her father and stepmother and baby half sister, Lily, had dulled Lisa's memory of what life with her mother had become since the divorce. Mrs. Atwood hadn't reacted well to the breakup of her marriage. She had always put a lot of energy into maintaining the illusion of a perfect home and a perfect family. Now that her illusion had been shattered, she was having trouble picking up the pieces and moving on. Even after all this time, she spent far too many evenings each week with her therapy group, complaining bitterly about how Mr. Atwood had ruined her life.

As a loving daughter, Lisa had found this very difficult to watch and even more difficult to live with. And nothing had changed with her return from California. Between coddling her mother by pretending to enjoy their marathon trips to the mall—shopping being one of the few activities that still seemed to give Mrs. Atwood any pleasure—and setting the house back in order after two months' worth of her mother's listless housekeeping, Lisa was exhausted. She welcomed the routine of school, with its specific and finite assignments.

There was one other adjustment that Lisa had

had to make. She'd had to get used to missing her family and friends on the West Coast. Part of her life was there now, and being away was hard. She missed seeing her father every day; she missed the warmth and friendship of her stepmother, Evelyn. Even more, she missed being there to watch Lily grow up.

Still, for every way that it was hard to be back, there were several ways that it was wonderful. One of the most difficult things about spending the summer in California had been leaving her friends and her boyfriend behind. In the few days she had been back, she had been so busy preparing for school that she hadn't had nearly enough time to hang out with them. That was why she was looking forward so much to the outing planned for Saturday. All of them had enjoyed their end-of-summer trail ride so thoroughly that they hadn't wanted to let it end, so they were extending the fun with a trail ride and barbecue for all their friends.

Of course, it won't be the same as it was back in the days when it was just the three of us, Lisa thought a bit wistfully. *I mean, I'm glad that Alex will be there, and Phil and A.J., too, but . . .*

Her mind skittered away from the thought before she could finish it. But she couldn't quite shake the topic of change from her mind. So much had changed this summer. Lisa herself had changed, of course—spending the entire summer in a different state, with different people and a different way of life, could do that to you. And Lisa wasn't sorry about that, since she was sure those changes had made her a better, more interesting, and more mature person.

But while she'd been changing out in California, things had been changing in Willow Creek as well, and Lisa wasn't nearly as thrilled about those changes. Some of them she had more or less expected. For instance, Max's two daughters seemed to have sprouted up almost overnight. That wasn't so different from Lily, who had grown an incredible amount in the two months Lisa had spent with her. But other changes had taken Lisa by surprise, such as returning to find that Prancer, the Thoroughbred mare she had ridden for years, was now a favorite with a whole new generation of Pine Hollow riders.

I suppose I should have seen that coming, Lisa told herself ruefully. *After all, Prancer belongs to Pine Hollow. And it isn't as if I've ever been her only rider, though I always spent so much time with her that it sometimes felt like it.*

Still, Lisa felt strange when she realized that others might feel just as proprietary about Prancer these days as she always had.

It's funny, she thought, tugging absently at her hair. *Even now, after a summer apart and all these reminders and everything, I still can't help thinking of Prancer as mine. All mine.* She bit her lip. *Sort of like my friends . . .*

TWO

"Take it easy, boy," Carole murmured under her breath. She steadied her hands on the reins, letting Starlight know that she was there to help him. "We're in no hurry here. Don't start rushing the fence. You know better than that."

Starlight seemed to understand. His pace steadied as he approached the low oxer Carole had set up in the middle of Pine Hollow's main schooling ring. Carole felt her horse's eagerness and attention as they came within a few strides of the fence.

"Here we go," she whispered. Her motions practiced and almost automatic, she leaned forward until the top half of her body was at an incline. At the same time, she shifted most of her weight from her seat onto the balls of her feet while keeping her legs close to her horse's side. A moment later, Starlight was airborne.

He landed lightly, and Carole settled smoothly back into her original position, smiling with pleasure. She signaled for Starlight to stop, then leaned forward to pat him soundly on his shiny neck.

"That was great, boy," she told him. "Just great."

She turned Starlight, preparing to leave the ring, and almost lost a stirrup in surprise when she saw Ben Marlow leaning on the gate watching her. *How does he do that?* she wondered, a little irritably. *Sometimes he just appears out of nowhere. It's creepy!*

She knew she wasn't being fair. The young stable hand's appearance was hardly a mystery—Carole had been so wrapped up in her work with Starlight that she probably wouldn't have noticed a comet crashing to earth in the next paddock, let alone a quiet guy like Ben stopping by the ring. But did he always have to stare at her with that solemn, intense expression? Did she always have to find herself wondering exactly what was going on behind those dark, brooding eyes?

She forced herself to smile as she rode toward him. "Hi, Ben," she said, pushing back a springy dark curl that had escaped from under her hard hat. "I haven't seen you all day."

He grunted faintly—a sound that often passed for conversation with Ben. But he did open the gate and hold it for her so that she could ride Starlight through. And he reached for Starlight's bridle and held him steady so that she could dismount.

Once her feet were on the ground again, Carole

took hold of the reins and Ben stepped back, seeming a bit uncomfortable. *Of course, that's probably at least partly my fault,* Carole thought, her mind wandering back a few weeks to the day when she'd suddenly realized that she knew next to nothing about Ben, even though the two of them had been working together for some time. She didn't know anything about his family, his past, even where he lived. That had nagged at her for a while, enough that she had impulsively decided to follow him home from the stable one night and put at least one question about him to rest. The plan hadn't worked out quite the way she'd hoped, though. She had seen Ben's home, a decrepit little place across town, but he had caught her following him. Carole had realized too late that to an intensely private, rather suspicious soul like Ben, her innocent curiosity had been akin to betrayal. Ever since that night, things hadn't been quite the same between them. *Not that things between us were ever particularly normal,* Carole reminded herself. Still, she felt bad about the incident. She had apologized, of course, but that didn't seem like enough, and she was still trying to figure out how to make it up to him.

"Max wants to see you," Ben said abruptly, interrupting Carole's thoughts.

Carole nodded. "Okay. Thanks," she said automatically.

But she hesitated before heading inside. There was something she wanted to do. Something that might help heal the rift that still lay between her and Ben. Maybe even something that could help Ben lighten up and have some fun. *After all the hard work he's put in around this place lately, he deserves it,* she told herself, wrapping Starlight's reins nervously around one hand and then the other.

That didn't mean this was going to be easy. Ben had never exactly been a natural conversationalist. And lately he had been more sullen than ever. Carole knew it was at least partly because he had just lost out on a college scholarship he'd been counting on. That didn't make his prickliness much easier to take, though.

She screwed up her courage and smiled at him tentatively. "Listen," she began. "I was just wondering . . . I mean, I thought maybe you . . . I mean—" She forced herself to stop and take a deep breath before continuing. "What I'm trying to say is, my friends and I are getting together on Saturday for a little picnic." Suddenly she wondered if calling it a picnic sounded too babyish or dorky. She gulped. "That is, we're going on a trail ride, and then we're going to have a sort of barbecue. There's this clearing in the woods near a deep water hole— well, you've ridden in the woods, so you probably know the place, but—" She paused for another breath. "Anyway. What I wanted to know was if you wanted to come along with us. It's Saturday. Did I say that already?"

Ben was staring at her. His mouth opened, then closed again. His expression was hard to read, as always, but it seemed to be some mixture of confusion, suspicion, and astonishment.

Suddenly Carole started to wonder if what she had said had come out wrong. She hadn't meant to imply . . . "A bunch of us are going," she added quickly, her face burning. She busied herself with removing her hard hat to hide her embarrassment. "Together. All of us, I mean. Stevie and Lisa and, well, Phil and Alex, and Phil's friend A.J.—I think you've met him a couple of times—and Callie, of course, and we invited Scott, but he—"

"Sorry," Ben interrupted. "Can't make it." With that, he spun on his heel and stalked off in the direction of the feed shed, a dark scowl on his face.

Carole stared after him, feeling a little hurt at his blunt reply. "Why do I keep trying with that guy?" she muttered to Starlight, who was munching on a mouthful of weeds he'd snitched from the edge of the ring while she wasn't paying attention. The horse simply gave her a wise look and continued chewing.

Carole sighed, tucked her hat under one arm, and led the gelding toward the stable door. She should have known that Ben wouldn't want to come along on Saturday. He had a truly special rapport with horses, but when it came to people, he wasn't exactly the king of social skills. He made a point of avoiding places where two people or more were gathered—except, sometimes, when those two people were Max and Carole. Even then, he never had much to say. On the other hand, he had come to a barbecue at the Foresters' house several weeks before and had seemed to enjoy himself. Still, that outing had been an exception.

Maybe I should just accept the simple truth, Carole told herself. *I'll never understand Ben, he'll never understand me, and that's that. We should just stick to business and forget about being friends.*

She did her best to put the whole subject out of her mind as she and her horse headed down the stable aisle. "And now," she said out loud, addressing Starlight again, "it's time to put you in your stall and go see what Max wants."

"Want a bite?" Alex scooped up some chocolate ice cream and whipped cream with his spoon and held it out.

Lisa leaned across the table and accepted the offering, closing her eyes as the rich chocolate melted on her tongue. "Mmm," she said with feeling. "This is wonderful."

"The ice cream?" Alex grinned at her devilishly.

She opened her eyes and stuck out her tongue at him. "Very funny," she said. "You know what I mean. You. Us. Being here together."

"I know." Alex leaned forward and gave her a quick, chocolatey kiss. Then he settled back to his ice cream once again. "Believe me, I was missing this all summer while you were gone. In a big way."

"Me too. I can still hardly believe we were apart for so long." Lisa took a sip of her vanilla milk shake. "So how was your first day of school?"

Alex rolled his eyes. "You know how it is at good old Fenton Hall. Same old teachers, same old kids . . ." He shrugged and licked his spoon.

"I always thought going to a private school like Fenton Hall would be kind of neat," Lisa said. "Those thick stone walls, the old leaded windows on the top floor—it's pretty romantic-looking, actually."

Alex shrugged. "I don't know about that," he said. "I don't think it can hold a candle to Willow Creek High in the romance department. After all, how can you call a school romantic when *you're* not there?"

"Easily," Lisa countered with a smile. "I can call it that because *you're* there." She loved this feeling— the comfortable feeling of joking around with her boyfriend, enjoying his company, relaxing completely into their warm, familiar relationship, and knowing that he understood her better than anyone else ever had before—that their love for each other was stronger, deeper, richer than she had ever believed possible. Lisa had always been an honest, caring person. But she had never opened up so completely to anyone before Alex. Not even her best friends, not even her family, knew her the way he did.

Alex grinned and settled back in his seat. "Well, if you'd gone there since kindergarten like I have, you'd realize that romantic-looking doesn't mean a thing. Fenton Hall is like any other school. It never changes."

Lisa rested her elbows on the table and looked around her. "Kind of like this place, huh?" They were sitting at their favorite table for two at TD's, an ice cream parlor in a small strip mall about a mile from Pine Hollow. Lisa and her friends had been going there for ages—it had once been a favorite spot for their Saddle Club meetings, which usually turned into hours-long gab sessions. Now it was a favorite place for Lisa to meet Alex in the afternoons, since it was convenient to their schools and their homes.

"That's different." Alex's gaze wandered over the glossy white walls and brightly colored booths of the small restaurant. "Places like this aren't supposed to change. Some things you just want to be able to count on."

"You can count on one thing for sure," she said lightly. "We're going to have fun on Saturday. Right?"

"Definitely." Alex's face brightened. "I can't wait. Out on the trail, in the woods, you and me . . ."

"And Carole, and Phil, and A.J., and Julianna," Lisa went on teasingly. "And don't forget your very own beloved twin sister, Stevie."

Alex let out a mock groan and covered his eyes with one hand. "Don't remind me," he said. "I sometimes think the only thing that isn't absolutely perfect about you is your taste in friends. Specifically, my crazy sister."

Lisa grinned, knowing he was kidding. Stevie and Alex had once spent most of their time fighting and playing elaborate practical jokes on each other. So had Stevie and her other brothers, Chad and Michael. But all four of the Lake siblings had matured over the past few years, and by now they had reached the point where they actually enjoyed one another's company most of the time. *Well, except maybe for Michael,* Lisa added to herself with a secret smile. *He's only thirteen, and it can't be easy for him, being the youngest in* that *wacky family!*

"Don't worry," she told Alex. "I'm sure Stevie

will be too busy hanging out with Phil to bother you. Much, anyway."

"Well, all I can say is that my darling sister isn't getting anywhere near the grill if I have anything to say about it," Alex joked. "The last time Stevie tried to cook a hamburger on my dad's grill by the pool, the outside ended up totally charred but the inside was still mooing."

"Stevie has many talents, but cooking has never been one of them," Lisa admitted. "Don't worry, though—I'll be in charge of the grill. We had a bunch of picnics on the beach over the summer, and I learned a few tricks I've been dying to show off."

"Really?" Alex was still smiling, but suddenly his eyes had taken on a slightly wary look, one that Lisa had come to recognize in the few days she'd been home. He hadn't wanted her to go to California, but she'd thought he understood why she'd had to go. Now he was acting weird about it. "Who taught you?"

"Evelyn," Lisa replied firmly, guessing what he was thinking. "She's a great cook, and she's been grilling since she was my age. She makes the best barbecued chicken I've ever tasted." *Why can't he get it through his head?* she thought with a twinge of annoyance. *I've told him often enough that Skye and I are just friends.*

She didn't like having to reassure him over and

over on that point. Yes, Skye Ransom was a famous, wealthy, handsome TV and movie star. Yes, Lisa had been friends with Skye for years. Yes, she had spent a lot of time with Skye over the summer while working as a stable hand on the set of his new show, *Paradise Ranch*. But as she had explained to Alex many times, that didn't mean he had anything to worry about. She was in love with Alex, not Skye.

"Well, that's great." Alex shrugged and glanced at his sundae. "I guess barbecues on the beach are just one more wonderful thing about life on the West Coast."

His words were normal, almost playful, but they still made Lisa's stomach contract. Why was it that anytime she said something about California, Alex seemed to withdraw from her a little?

She concentrated on her milk shake, trying to figure it out. It couldn't just be jealousy about Skye. Could it? Sure, Alex had seemed pretty insecure about that while she was actually in California. She had understood that, or at least accepted it. But now she was back. They were together. And he could see—or he should be able to see—that she was just as devoted to him as she had been before she left. The summer was over.

Or maybe it wasn't over, not really. Maybe she was asking too much when she expected Alex to simply forget about the time they had spent apart and move on. After all, it wasn't as if Lisa herself had forgotten those two months. On the contrary, she cherished the memory of them.

Maybe that's it, she told herself. *Maybe what's making Alex jealous and weird isn't Skye at all. Maybe it's the whole idea of my going to California in the first place, of leaving him behind for the whole summer.*

That was a new thought, and one that made her more than a little uncomfortable. She still hadn't told Alex how close she'd come to staying in California after the end of the summer—going to school there, living with her father. She had planned to share her thoughts with him, as she had with Stevie and Carole, but so far the right moment hadn't presented itself. Now she wondered if it ever would.

I knew he didn't want me to go, she thought. *But I never considered that he might actually* resent *it.*

She decided to test her new theory. "California is a pretty cool place," she said carefully. "It's really different from Virginia. I'm glad I got to try living there. Even though it was really hard to leave my life here for two whole months. Especially you."

Alex shrugged. "Whatever. You're back now, and that's what matters." He paused and wiped chocolate off his chin with a paper napkin. "So anyway, did you check with Max about a horse for me to ride on Saturday?"

Lisa held back a sigh. It seemed that her theory was right. *He still doesn't get it,* she thought in despair. *He doesn't understand how I could voluntarily leave him behind for two months. He doesn't even want to talk about it. But if he doesn't understand why I went, how will he ever understand everything that my time in California taught me? How will he still be able to really understand* me?

Realizing that Alex was waiting for her to speak, Lisa forced herself to smile as if nothing were wrong. *Nothing* is *wrong,* she told herself firmly. *Even the best couples don't have to share every single thought and feeling they have. The most important thing right now is to reassure Alex—make him realize how important he is to me. And if that means not talking about California with him, so be it. It's not that big a deal. I'm sure we'll be able to discuss it someday, after we've both had some time to readjust.*

"I think you're going to be riding Congo on Saturday," she told Alex. "Max says you've improved a lot lately. Actually, he said something about how living with Stevie all these years must have finally rubbed off on you."

"Hey," Alex protested, pretending to pout. "That wasn't very nice of him. The part about Stevie, I mean."

Lisa giggled, though it felt a bit forced. *Stop it,* she told herself sternly. *This is Alex you're talking to, remember? Nothing has changed.*

But deep in her heart, she couldn't help thinking that for the first time since they'd fallen in love, something *had* changed between them. And she wasn't quite sure how to fix it.

THREE

As Lisa pulled into the driveway of Pine Hollow on Saturday morning, she spotted Carole turning in right behind her. Coasting into a spot in the parking area under the shade of a large oak tree, she cut the ignition, hopped out of the car, and retrieved a bagful of picnic supplies from her trunk. By the time she had closed the trunk, Carole was climbing out of her own car.

"Well, we survived our first week of school!" Lisa called to Carole.

Carole groaned as she reached into her backseat and grabbed her backpack. "Just barely," she said. "I'm trying to convince Dad to lend me his mobile phone during the school day. I figure I might need it to call nine-one-one if I start to die of boredom."

Lisa laughed. "Maybe you should skip the phone and just get one of those medical alert devices," she teased. "You know, the kind that gives you a direct hookup to the paramedics. 'Help! I've fallen asleep and I can't wake up!' "

Lisa had long since accepted the fact that she and her two best friends would never agree on some things. One of those things was schoolwork. Stevie had always been the least serious of the three when it came to classes and grades, often just sliding by. Lisa had never quite understood that, since Stevie's quick and creative mind should have guaranteed her straight A's with only minimum effort.

As for Carole, she had always seemed to regard schoolwork as a necessary evil—although lately, Lisa had noticed, she was starting to stress the *evil* part a lot more than the *necessary* part. School had always seemed a little like the place Carole stopped between home and the stable, and these days that was truer than ever.

Lisa herself had always done very well in school, earning a long and almost unbroken series of A's along with numerous academic honors. She was aware that her friends thought her good grades were primarily the result of her perfectionism, and that had certainly been a part of it. But there was a little more to it than that. Earning good grades, learning new things, and keeping her teachers' approval had always been a real source of comfort and pride to Lisa, much the way Carole's work at the stable and love of horses were to her.

"Most of my classes seem pretty interesting, now that my teachers have finally started teaching," Lisa said, leading the way toward the stable entrance. "But I have to admit, I'm glad the weekend is here. I'm looking forward to spending a whole day's worth of quality time with Prancer."

"Prancer?" Carole repeated.

Lisa shot her an amused look. "Yeah, you know, Prancer. Prancer, the horse I've been riding for the last few years. I was gone so long that I'm afraid she's forgotten who I am!"

"No way," Carole said loyally. She paused, then went on. "Actually, though, I was thinking about something on my way over."

"What?" Lisa asked absently. She had gone back to thinking about her friends' strange attitudes toward school. It never ceased to amaze her that the three of them could have been so close for so many years and yet be such totally different people in some ways. *Still, I guess we've always had one thing in common,* she thought. *We all feel the same way about horses.*

Carole hesitated. "Well, you know Calypso?"

"Of course."

"I was just wondering if you might consider, um, riding her today. Instead of Prancer."

Lisa furrowed her brow, her attention finally focused on her friend. "Why would I want to do that?" Hadn't Carole been listening to what she had said just now about spending time with Prancer?

Carole shrugged, looking slightly uncomfortable. "It's just that Max was saying the other day that Calypso could use some more trail experience. I mean, he's bred her almost every year since he bought her, so she hasn't been ridden as much as some of the other horses. And she's such a nice horse, it would be great if he could start using her more in classes and stuff. I just thought you might like to help out—you know, especially since Calypso is a pretty Thoroughbred mare, just like Prancer. You two would probably get along great."

Lisa waved her hands. "Wait," she commanded. "Are my ears deceiving me? Are you—you, Carole Hanson, of all people—actually trying to convince me to give up a ride on the horse I've been missing like crazy all summer? The horse I've only had a chance to ride once—that's one lousy time—since I got back? What's the deal?"

"Nothing, forget it," Carole said quickly. "Never mind. It was just a thought. A dumb idea. I'll work with Calypso myself next week."

Lisa shrugged. "Okay," she said, giving Carole one last puzzled look. But she didn't think about her friend's silly suggestion for long. She was too busy looking forward to starting their ride—on her favorite horse in the whole world, Prancer.

". . . so I told Max you should probably ride Nickel today," Stevie told Phil. "That way, when you fall off every few steps, it's not such a long way to the ground."

"Funny." Phil grinned and leaned on the half door of the stall. "Did you also tell him that I'm planning to lose you in the woods so I can find myself a girlfriend who doesn't make fun of me all the time?"

Inside the stall, Stevie smoothed the hair on the broad back of her horse, a feisty bay mare named Belle. "Nope," she replied seriously. "That's not going to happen. You're too much fun to make fun of. No girl could resist. You should just be glad that my quips are always so witty and clever." She grinned at him briefly, then turned her attention back to Belle. "Hand me the saddle pad, will you?" She gestured toward Belle's green fabric saddle pad, which she had hung over the stall door atop her well-worn leather saddle.

"Fine." Phil grabbed the saddle pad and held it behind his back. "But not unless you admit that I'm the best rider in the entire known universe and give me a kiss to prove you mean it."

Stevie pretended to pout, but she walked over and kissed him lightly on the lips. "There's your kiss," she said. "As for the other part, forget it. Now hand it over."

Phil pretended to hesitate, but then he took a step into the stall and held out the saddle pad. When Stevie reached to take it, Phil grabbed her hand and planted a big, wet, noisy kiss right in the middle of her palm.

"Ick." Stevie giggled. "I just cleaned out Belle's feet with that hand."

"Really?" Phil raised one eyebrow and licked his lips. "Well, her hooves are just divine. Wanna taste?" With that, he grabbed her and planted another kiss right on her mouth.

She broke away quickly and wiped her mouth, pretending to be disgusted but hardly able to stop laughing.

When Stevie thought about how many years she had been kissing Phil, it sometimes amazed her. To most people their age, Stevie and Phil's three-year relationship was more than an oddity—it was virtually unique. Stevie herself could hardly remember a time when they hadn't been together. But to her, that didn't seem strange at all. From the moment she had met Phil at riding camp the summer they were both thirteen, the world had suddenly seemed brighter and even more fun. He had always known how to make her laugh, and unlike a lot of guys, he also understood when she occasionally needed to cry or yell.

I really am lucky to have him, she thought with satisfaction as she smoothed the saddle pad over Belle's withers. She glanced at him out of the corner of her eye. He didn't notice, since he was busy searching his jeans pockets for something. *And I'm doubly lucky that such a great guy also happens to be totally cute!*

"Uh-oh," Phil muttered. He patted his back pockets, then dug into his front ones again, looking slightly perturbed.

Stevie stepped over to pick up Belle's saddle. "What's the matter?" she asked, pausing at the stall door.

"My wallet. I think I left it in the locker room while we were changing shoes."

Stevie wrinkled her nose. "You needed to take out your wallet to change into your boots?"

"Ha ha," Phil tossed over his shoulder. He was already heading down the aisle in the direction of the locker room. "I took it out to give you that article I saved for you about the dressage entries for the Colesford Horse Show, remember? So if someone steals my whole wallet, it'll be all your fault."

Stevie just grinned as her boyfriend disappeared around the corner at the end of the aisle. She knew there was little chance of Phil's wallet being stolen—not at Pine Hollow. The worst that would happen would be that Max's daughters' puppy might find it and chew on it a little.

She returned her attention to Belle, settling the saddle on her back and going through the familiar motions of securing it. A few minutes later Belle's bridle was on, too. And Phil still hadn't returned.

"What's taking him so long?" Stevie asked her horse.

Belle stared at her owner blankly, then reached forward to nibble at a loose strand of Stevie's dark blond hair. Stevie giggled.

"Quit it, you monster." She pushed the horse away. Then she let herself out of the stall and glanced down the aisle. There was still no sign of Phil. "Oh well," Stevie told Belle. "He's probably taking his time because he's hoping I'll be so impatient to get started that I'll decide to tack up Barq for him while he's gone." She shrugged and sighed, giving Belle one last pat." And I guess he's right."

Stevie was just fastening the noseband on Barq's bridle when Phil finally hurried down the aisle, flushed and breathless.

"There you are," she said sardonically. "Did you get lost? Or were you just hoping I'd get so bored I'd tack up your horse for you?"

Phil shot her a sheepish grin as he opened the

stall door and stepped forward to take Barq's lead. "Sorry about that," he said. "It only took me a second to find my wallet—it was lying right there on the bench where I left it. But Scott Forester was in the locker room, and we got to talking."

"Scott? You were talking to Scott all this time?" Stevie frowned. She knew that Phil had met Scott several times over the summer. He had even attended a party at the Foresters' house a few weeks ago. But as far as she had noticed, the two boys had never exchanged more than a polite hello and small talk.

"Sure. He was here dropping Callie off." Phil clucked to Barq and led him down the aisle to Belle's stall, where Stevie ducked in to retrieve her horse. "I tried to convince him to come along with us today—I mean, he's got to be at least as good a rider as your brother, right?—but he has some kind of debate society meeting this afternoon, so he begged off."

"No kidding," Stevie said, leading Belle into the aisle and latching the stall door behind her. "He wouldn't be caught dead at any gathering I was a part of. He might actually be forced to talk to me or something."

Phil shot her a sympathetic look. "I don't know, Stevie," he said as the two of them led their horses down the aisle at a leisurely walk. "I know you two have had some tough times this summer. But Scott seems like a pretty cool guy. His head's in the right place, you know? And didn't you say you thought he might be warming up to you a little?"

"I thought so," Stevie muttered. "But now I think I was wrong."

She didn't bother to go into details, but she was thinking of chemistry class. She and Scott didn't sit anywhere near each other, so there was no real reason he would talk to her before class. Still, she couldn't help noticing that, like the future politician he undoubtedly was, Scott had already sought out the acquaintance of just about every other person in the class. *Except me,* she thought sourly. *He already made my acquaintance. And now he doesn't want it anymore.*

She wondered what Scott and Phil had found to talk about for so long, but she shied away from asking Phil. It was too weird to think about the two of them hanging out in the locker room, chatting away together without her there to hear what they were saying. Had her name come up? If so, what had they said? How had Scott reacted? Was Phil telling the truth about Scott's response to his invitation, or had Scott actually said something else? Something about not wanting to spend time with Stevie? Phil might have changed the story to spare her feelings.

At heart, Stevie was an optimist. *Maybe this will turn out to be a good thing,* she told herself. *If Scott warms up to Phil, maybe he'll warm up to me again, too. After all, something has to give between us sooner or later, right? We go to the same school, we both spend a lot of time at Pine Hollow—we can't spend the entire year not talking to each other.*

Can we?

FOUR

Carole was feeling good as their group rode away from Pine Hollow a short while later. It was a perfect September day—warm and sunny, but without the oppressive heat and humidity that frequently came along with late summer in northern Virginia. Starlight was feeling frisky, his mouth exploring the bit and his tail swishing energetically at the occasional fly. The grass in the pasture they were approaching was lush and green, thanks to recent rains, and even the stable yard seemed less hot and dusty than usual as they crossed it. School felt a million miles away.

If only it were a million years away, too, Carole thought. *Then everything really would be perfect!*

She smiled ruefully at the thought. She brought Starlight to a halt as Stevie, who was in the lead with Phil, reached the pasture fence.

"I'll get the gate," Stevie called, steering Belle closer so that she could reach the latch.

As she waited, Carole turned to check on Lisa, who was a short distance behind her. It was Lisa's turn to lead Patch, who was serving as a packhorse on this trip, carrying the supplies for the barbecue in the packsaddle.

Lisa and Patch were fine. The gelding, standing lazily beside Calypso, looked small and a bit stumpy next to the long-legged, elegant Thoroughbred. Lisa didn't seem to be having any trouble with Calypso, the high-spirited but obliging chestnut mare, but Carole still felt a little bit guilty when she glanced at Lisa's face. Lisa had clearly been annoyed when she had arrived at Prancer's stall and found that the mare wasn't there. Carole hadn't been sure what to say. Luckily, Red O'Malley had come to the rescue. The head stable hand had muttered something about a rabies booster shot and a reshoeing, which would keep Prancer tied up for the next hour or so. Lisa had seemed disappointed but not suspicious, which wasn't surprising, considering that she had been far away in California a month earlier when Carole had helped the vet administer Prancer's real rabies shot. *Come to think of it, that should have tipped me off to what was going on,* Carole told herself ruefully. *Lisa probably can't even guess the truth.*

At the moment, Lisa was chatting easily with A.J., who was riding beside her on Comanche, another Pine Hollow stable horse. A.J. and Phil both had their own horses, but they hadn't bothered to van them over to Pine Hollow for this outing. Instead they had hired horses from Max for the day. Carole couldn't help smiling as she took in the sight of A.J. and Comanche together. The chestnut gelding's deep, reddish brown coat matched A.J.'s dark auburn hair almost perfectly. Carole also noticed that A.J. was keeping an eye on his girlfriend, a pretty, petite redhead named Julianna, even as he talked to Lisa. Carole knew that Julianna had only been riding as long as she'd been dating A.J.—in other words, less than four months. But she looked quite comfortable aboard Chip, the even-tempered Appaloosa Carole had selected for her that day. That wasn't surprising. Julianna had the uncanny talent of seeming comfortable in almost any situation. Carole envied her that ability.

Carole was about to turn her attention back to the gate ahead of them when a slight movement caught her eye. It was coming from the stable entrance some fifty yards back.

Carole squinted, trying to make out the figure that was partially hidden in the shadows cast over the doorway by the strong late-morning sunshine. *That looks like Ben,* she thought. *But what's he doing?* It definitely wasn't like the hardworking stable hand to stand around when there were chores to be done. And Carole had been riding long enough to know that there were *always* stable chores to be done.

A second later, the figure melted away into the stable interior, and Carole shook her head, uncertain that Ben had ever been there, watching them ride off. Before she could think about it any further, she became aware that another horse and rider were moving toward her.

Turning to face forward again, she saw that Callie was approaching on a palomino named PC. The well-trained gelding belonged to a girl named Emily Williams who also rode at Pine Hollow. Carole, Stevie, and Lisa had known Emily for years, and she had become such a good friend that they hardly even remembered that Emily had cerebral palsy and couldn't walk without crutches. That may have been because when Emily was in the saddle, she rode every bit as well as any of them—partly thanks to PC. The good-natured palomino had received training that allowed Emily to control him by special aids that didn't require much use of her legs.

Emily was accomplished enough as a rider these days that she occasionally rode horses other than PC. The girls had invited her along on today's excursion, but she had made plans with other friends and had to decline. Carole wondered if that was making Callie nervous at all—Emily had been Callie's constant riding coach and adviser since the accident, and her insight had helped Callie a lot. Then again, Carole decided, Callie wasn't the type of person to let nerves stop her from doing anything she wanted. That was one reason she had been a successful endurance rider before her accident—and also why she was making such strong and steady progress in her recovery.

"Hi." Callie steered PC around until he was standing beside Starlight. "I'm really glad you guys came up with this idea. I've been dying to get back out on a trail for ages. But I doubt my parents would have approved of any trail ride short of one that involved a whole cavalry, like this." She waved a hand to indicate the six other riders surrounding them.

Stevie had the gate open by now, and Carole nudged Starlight toward it at a walk. "Glad we could help." She turned and smiled at Callie, who was riding beside her. "I know it's not exactly a hundred-mile endurance competition, but hey, you have to start somewhere, right?"

"You got it." Callie paused, holding PC back so that Carole could pass through the gate ahead of her. Once they were through, she caught up again to continue their conversation. "Sometimes I think the hardest thing about being injured is being out of training for so long."

Carole nodded sympathetically. "That must be

really frustrating," she said. "But with your determination, you'll make up for lost ground quickly. I'm sure of it."

"Thanks." Callie smiled, looking pleased.

Carole smiled back, thinking how quickly Callie had become a part of life at Pine Hollow. Carole and Callie hadn't hit it off right away, thanks to a few silly little misunderstandings, but once they had come to know each other, they had gotten along fine. Both were serious about horses and riding, and that had helped them overcome the initial awkwardness between them. These days Carole could no more imagine life at the stable without Callie than—well, than she could imagine it without Stevie or Lisa. Or Max. Or Starlight.

She leaned forward to pat her horse as the group started across the wide pasture and toward the woods on the far side. "So how was your first week at Fenton Hall?" she asked Callie.

Callie shrugged. "You know how it is. Going to a new school is hard."

Carole could relate to that. Before moving to Willow Creek, her family had moved around a lot because of her father's military job. "I know," she told Callie. "At least Stevie was there, though. And your brother."

Callie knew that Carole was trying to help, but the last thing she felt like talking about was school.

She knew she would settle in at Fenton Hall eventually, maybe even make some new friends. But she also knew it would take time. She could blame it on her crutches and her slow and awkward walk if she wanted to, but the truth was, she simply didn't have Scott's almost magical talent for instantly connecting with people. There had always been that difference between them. Scott could walk into a room full of a dozen strangers and walk out ten minutes later with a dozen lifelong pals, while Callie had trouble finding anything to say to any new acquaintance, no matter how friendly. That was why she cherished the new friends she had made at Pine Hollow. Just being at the stable made getting to know people a lot easier for her, since horses were the one topic Callie never had any trouble discussing. Once she had gotten to know Stevie and Carole and some of the other riders at Pine Hollow, their horse chat had slid naturally into friendship, even in the midst of all the hard work and heartache that had followed the accident early in the summer.

As for school—well, Callie would have to be a little more patient there, and she wasn't particularly good at being patient. So for now she was doing her best not to think too much about it when she didn't have to.

She wasn't sure Carole would understand that, though—friendly, down-to-earth Carole, who even managed somehow to coax conversation and friendship out of taciturn Ben Marlow—so she decided to change the subject instead of trying to explain.

"I heard you finally had your big job talk with Max the other day," Callie said, letting PC fall into an even walk beside Starlight. "Stevie said he talked to you about changing your duties now that you're coming in part-time. What did he have to say?"

"He wants me to have the chance to learn everything," Carole said. "He even said something about wanting me to take on more responsibility for training some of the younger horses at Pine Hollow."

"You mean like Firefly?" Callie said, thinking of the flashy young mare Max had recently bought.

Carole nodded. "Ben and I have already been working with her. I guess Max thinks we've been doing okay at that, because he said he wants me to take on another project or two. He seems to be taking the start of our new school year as an opportunity to restructure some of his training schedules or something." She smiled and shrugged. "He said he had a couple of specific horses in mind for me to take over, but he wasn't ready to tell me which ones yet."

Callie chuckled. Max Regnery had his quirks, but he really knew what he was doing with his horses. She said as much to Carole, adding, "I'm sure he'll let you in on the secret soon enough."

"I'm sure he will." Carole forced herself to keep smiling. But Callie's words had just reminded her of another secret—a secret Carole still wasn't sure she would be able to keep. It would be nice to talk about it with Callie—capable, coolheaded Callie, who might actually have some ideas about . . .

But no. Carole had made a promise to Max, and she intended to honor it and keep his secret. No matter how difficult that was turning out to be.

"Are you okay over there?" Lisa asked Alex, who was riding beside her on a big warmblood gelding named Congo. "Or do you want to ride in front of me on my saddle, where you'll be less likely to fall off?"

"Very funny," Alex retorted with a grin. "I'd be happy to ride in front of you. But it would have nothing to do with falling off."

Lisa giggled. She glanced away from Alex long enough to check on Patch, who was moving along obediently beside her horse. Then she looked over at her boyfriend again. "We'd better save that kind of stuff for our own private trail ride," she said. "But seriously, I was just kidding. You must have had time for a few more lessons in between all those lawn jobs you had this summer. It shows." It still gave her a warm glow when she thought of the day, less than a month into their relationship, when Alex had told her he wanted to learn to ride. Lisa had been surprised, to say the least. When she had first become friends with Stevie, Alex had delighted in taking every opportunity to tease his twin about her obsession with horses. But once he fell in love with Lisa, Alex had wanted to explore everything that mattered to her, and that included riding. Lisa understood perfectly—she felt the same way about his interests. She knew that Alex would never be quite as enthusiastic as she was about riding, just as she would never get quite as excited as he did about in-line skating or soccer. But spending more time learning about each other's favorite activities really didn't seem like a sacrifice to either of them. It just gave them more ways to be together.

"I may have stopped by Pine Hollow a few times on my days off," Alex admitted. "Mostly because it reminded me of you, of course. But you know Max—if I was going to hang around, I either had to ride or spend all my time shoveling manure. Naturally, I chose to ride." He grinned. "Actually, I'm probably as good as you are by now. It just doesn't show because you're on that fancy Thoroughbred."

Lisa smiled weakly at his joke. *That's right,* she thought. *I'm riding a Thoroughbred. Just not the Thoroughbred I wanted to ride.* She still couldn't believe her bad luck. She also couldn't help feeling a little annoyed at Max. *Since when does he schedule immunizations on Saturdays, anyway?* she thought grumpily. Then she reminded herself that Red had also said something about Prancer throwing a shoe. That was something even Max couldn't have prevented, and Lisa knew it, so she was riding Calypso after all. She was disappointed, but Calypso was a perfectly nice horse. And Lisa would have plenty of other opportunities to get reacquainted with Prancer.

"I don't know about that," she countered as she and Alex left the sunny pasture for the cool, dappled shade of a wooded trail. There was just enough room for the two of them to ride beside each other, with Patch tagging along at Calypso's flank. "Congo's kind of bashful, so he may not have told you, but one of Max's younger riders took a blue ribbon with him at a show just last spring. So I'm afraid you've got no excuse."

Alex didn't have a response to that, so he just stuck out his tongue and crossed his eyes, making Lisa laugh. After that, the two rode side by side through the woods in a comfortable silence, broken only occasionally by shouts of laughter drifting back from A.J., Phil, and Julianna, who were riding ahead of them.

A few minutes later, as the trail widened slightly, Phil pulled up and waited for Lisa and Alex to come even with him before signaling for Barq to walk again. "Hey," he greeted them. "Are you tired of leading Patch yet, Lisa? I'll take a turn if you want."

"Thanks." Lisa relinquished Patch's lead to Phil. As he and Alex started to chat about the team standings in some sport or other, she glanced forward. Now that she was free of leading duty, maybe she would leave the two guys together and catch up to Carole and Stevie, who were both riding farther ahead in the group. The three of them hadn't had much time alone together since Lisa's return from California, and they still had some catching up to do. The trail was winding around at the moment and Lisa couldn't see either of her friends—or anyone else aside from A.J. and Julianna—but she, Alex, and Phil were bringing up the rear, so she knew that Carole and Stevie were ahead of her somewhere.

She was on the verge of asking Calypso to trot when she rounded a corner and found a wide, straight, smooth stretch of trail ahead. She also found that the entire group was now in view.

Callie and Stevie were leading the way. They were obviously having a conversation, though Lisa was too far back to hear what they were saying. As Lisa watched, Stevie suddenly urged Belle into a brisk trot. With a shriek of laughter, Callie followed suit on PC. Before long, the two of them were dueling it out in an impromptu trotting race along the shady path. Carole, who had been riding just behind them, joined in gamely, letting out a gleeful *"Yeee-ha!"* and putting Starlight into a canter. When he caught up with the others she moved him back into his long, swinging trot.

Soon the three racers were far ahead of the rest of the pack. After a moment, they disappeared around another bend in the trail, out of Lisa's sight.

It wasn't until Calypso shook her head vehemently that Lisa realized she was clutching the reins tightly in both hands, pulling back on the mare's mouth. She quickly loosened her grip and gave the horse an apologetic pat. But her gaze remained focused on the spot ahead where her two best friends—and Callie—had just disappeared.

They've really gotten close to Callie this summer, she thought, her throat suddenly feeling tight. *I guess that's only natural.*

Natural though it might have been, Lisa had to admit that she wasn't thrilled about it. This was perhaps the most serious change that had occurred in her absence. Carole and Stevie had spent the entire summer getting to know Callie, working with her on her physical therapy, introducing her to Pine Hollow and Willow Creek. Lisa had met the new girl before she left, but she had been distracted by thoughts of her upcoming trip, so the two of them hadn't had much time to really get acquainted.

And now Callie seemed to be an accepted part of their tight-knit group, every bit as comfortable with Lisa's best friends as Alex and Phil were. *I wasn't expecting that at all,* Lisa thought, admitting it to herself for the first time. *Especially after the rocky start she and Carole had. How could they ever end up friends after all that? And the accident—Stevie was so torn up about what happened, how could she and Callie have come through it with a normal relationship?*

But somehow it had happened. And now Lisa was left in the uncomfortable position of playing catch-up, trying to find her place in a group of friends that had expanded and changed without her. It wasn't that she disliked Callie—in fact, she found her smart and interesting. But she didn't feel that she knew her well enough to want to share Carole and Stevie with her. Not yet. It was an awkward situation, and even though Lisa was sure that her friends didn't have the slightest clue about how she was feeling—how could they, if she didn't say anything about it?—she couldn't help feeling a twinge of annoyance with them for leaving her behind.

That's not fair, she scolded herself. *You were the one who went away for the summer. What were they supposed to do? Ignore Callie until you got home and gave them permission to be friends with her?*

For once Lisa's logical thoughts weren't much comfort. The three of them had been best friends for so long, and until her return Lisa hadn't had a clue that anything had changed. Her friends had barely mentioned Callie's name during their visit to California just before her return.

Never mind about that, she told herself, urging Calypso into a trot as she reached the smooth part of the trail. The mare's easy, limber gait reminded her of Prancer, and she sighed. *Life is about change, right? Like it or not, nothing seems to stay the same for very long, and all we can do is figure out how to deal with it. I figured that out this summer. I'll just have to adjust to this change, too—somehow.*

FIVE

"Don't you think you should get the food closer to the coals?" Stevie said helpfully. "Otherwise it'll take forever to cook."

Phil cocked an eyebrow at her. "To cook? Or to burn?" he teased.

Callie laughed. "I've heard plenty of stories about your way with a burger, Stevie," she said. "In fact, on our ride here, Alex made me swear not to let you near a spatula or he'd go on a hunger strike."

"He could use one," Stevie replied tartly. "All that ice cream he and Lisa have been eating since she got back is going to make him fat." She knew it was a ridiculous accusation, since Alex had always been as thin as a rail. Actually, he had shot up at least six inches in the past couple of years, while his weight had remained fairly steady, so Stevie thought he looked more gangly than ever.

"Fine," Phil said soothingly. "But seriously,

Stevie, shoo. Callie and I have everything under control here. You might as well go for a swim."

For a second Stevie toyed with the idea of getting annoyed with Phil and Callie. Since when did they believe anything Alex said? She hadn't burned a burger on the grill for years. Of course, her father hadn't let her near the grill in years, either, but she was sure she would be much better at it now if they would only let her try.

As she glanced around her, though, she decided that arguing with them would be a waste—she would rather spend her time enjoying herself.

After riding through the woods for the better part of an hour, the group had reached the picnic site. If Stevie had planned it herself, she didn't think she could have designed this charming little spot in the woods any better. A deep, clean swimming hole formed by a sharp bend and a natural dam in Willow Creek lay a few yards ahead of her, just beyond the wide, sunny clearing where Phil had set up the grill. Deep woodland surrounded the swimming hole on three sides, while the fourth opened up into a grassy meadow dotted with late-summer wildflowers, where the horses were grazing contentedly.

Callie looked up from the coals and gave Stevie a searching look, obviously concerned about her silence. "You don't really want to cook, do you?" she asked, wiping a bead of sweat from her forehead. "I mean, I just thought I might as well do it because I can't swim." She gestured at her crutches, which had come along in Patch's packsaddle and were now leaning against a tree stump.

Stevie shot her a reassuring grin. "I know. And I'm glad you're being such a good sport about it," she said, quickly kicking off her boots and peeling her T-shirt over her head, revealing the faded cotton bathing suit she was wearing underneath. "Because I can't wait to get into that nice, cool water. See you!" Shedding her socks and jeans, Stevie raced toward the edge of the water and executed a perfect cannonball off the overhanging rock ledge that formed a natural diving platform above the deepest water.

Carole, for one, hardly noticed Stevie's dramatic entrance. She was too busy trying to hold her own in a three-way splash fight with A.J. and Julianna. The three of them were at the far end of the swimming hole, where the water was only about four feet deep.

"Ye shall never leave zis water hole alive!" A.J. shouted in an excruciatingly bad French accent. At the same time, he swept his arm along the surface of the swimming hole, sending a sheet of water cascading over both Carole and Julianna.

Julianna let out a shriek, windmilling her arms to try to avoid the onslaught and simultaneously getting both girls even wetter. She turned to Carole.

"What do you think?" she asked breathlessly, shaking her reddish gold bangs out of her eyes. "Girls against guy?"

"You're on," Carole agreed quickly.

A.J. was already swimming away, bent on escape. "You'll never take me alive!" he cried, letting out a loud shriek of diabolical laughter that ended with a gurgle as he dived underwater and shot across the swimming hole.

"Not so fast, buddy," Julianna cried, taking off after him.

Carole dived into the deeper water in hot pursuit, kicking hard and following the sounds of A.J.'s playful shouts and Julianna's giggles. She was having lots of fun, as everyone always seemed to whenever A.J. was around.

A.J. and Phil had been best friends for as long as the girls had known them. The two guys shared a love of riding and attended the same school, but those weren't the only things that made them so compatible. They also shared a lively, adventurous sense of humor and the unfailing ability to find fun in almost any situation.

Carole gave one last strong kick, opening her eyes under the murky water. She spotted a pale foot kicking away in front of her and grabbed it, thinking it belonged to A.J. It wasn't until she heard a squeal of dismay that she realized her mistake.

"Oops," she said, surfacing and treading water as she wiped her eyes. "Sorry about that, Julianna."

Julianna just giggled in reply. "Never mind," she said. "He was getting away anyway. At least now I have an excuse." She tugged at one shoulder strap of her bright red—and rather skimpy—bikini, drawing Carole's slightly envious eye.

Julianna really is gorgeous, she thought, glancing up from the other girl's figure to her pretty, heart-shaped face and wide-set, greenish blue eyes. *It's no wonder A.J. is so crazy about her.*

Still, Carole suspected that it wasn't just Julianna's looks that had drawn A.J.'s attention. Julianna had a bright, sunny, adaptable personality, which Carole and her friends agreed made a good match for A.J.'s sometimes goofy sense of humor.

Despite all that, Carole couldn't help wondering occasionally if Julianna was really the perfect girl for A.J. He certainly seemed to think so—in fact, he seemed to consider it a distinct honor that she had deigned to go out with him. Still, in Carole's opinion Julianna could sometimes come across as . . . well, perhaps a tad shallow. Not quite as sensitive as she ought to be. Even a bit careless in her comments and opinions.

However, there was no denying that Julianna could be a whole lot of fun at times like this, Carole reminded herself as the two girls continued to tread water, resting from their wild race across the swimming hole.

And if she makes him happy, I'm happy for him, Carole told herself firmly.

"Come on," Julianna urged Carole eagerly. "My half brother is on the wrestling team at his school, and he taught me a couple of grips last time I visited. If you help me catch A.J., I'll give them a try." She giggled. "Then we'll have him right where we want him."

Carole laughed. "Sorry," she said. "I have to pass this time. I'm all worn out."

Julianna didn't seem the least bit perturbed. "Okay, then I'll see you," she said, stroking off after A.J., who was making faces at them from the opposite end of the swimming hole. "Wish me luck!"

Carole waved her off, then turned to swim more slowly back toward the shallows nearby. She was still thinking about Julianna. *Maybe she's not perfect,* she mused. *But then again, who is? And if you have to have a fault, being too fun-loving is a pretty decent one to have. I can think of a few people who could stand to have a little bit of Julianna's friendliness and high spirits rub off on them.*

Before she could stop it, a picture of Ben Marlow flashed into her mind. She remembered how he had looked as he stood there in the shadows, watching their happy party ride off together. She had been too far away to get a good look at his face, but she had no trouble picturing the serious, almost grim expression he usually wore whenever he wasn't working with a horse. Why couldn't he ever just lighten up and let himself have fun?

Twenty minutes later, the enticing smell of cooking burgers was floating over the swimming hole. Lisa's stomach rumbled in anticipation as she floated on her back with her eyes closed, enjoying the warmth of the sun beating down on her. The day had grown hotter, but the water in the swimming hole was still cool and refreshing.

Lisa opened her eyes and allowed her legs to drop down until she was treading water. Wiping a few droplets out of her lashes, she glanced at the shore to see how the cooking was coming, wondering if she should volunteer to help. Lisa was a pretty good cook, and as she had told Alex, she had picked up some useful grilling tips from Evelyn that summer. It would be fun to try them out. But she saw that most of the burgers were already ready and waiting, piled high on a paper plate. As Lisa watched, Callie flipped another one expertly onto the pile. Then she and Phil set about slicing the buns they had brought and placing them on the grill to toast.

Looks like I'm not needed, Lisa thought with a

touch of self-pity. *Callie has everything under control. As usual.*

Then she chided herself for the uncharitable thought. Of course Callie was busy with the cooking. She was the only one of the party who couldn't swim. She hadn't even bothered to bring along a bathing suit. What else did she have to do?

Actually, knowing Callie, she could probably swim just fine, Lisa realized. *At least in the shallow area, where she wouldn't have to kick too much. After all, Carole told me Callie's been swimming in the family pool since her bandages came off.* But Lisa also knew that Callie's parents had forbidden her to do any swimming that day as a condition of their daughter's coming along on the ride. They were afraid that splashing around in a swimming hole full of rocks and weeds and other unexpected obstacles could be too dangerous. They were probably being overly cautious, and Lisa couldn't help feeling a twinge of sympathy for Callie. Her own mother could be the same way.

As she watched, Phil leaned over to say something to Callie, then turned and strolled off in the direction of the meadow. Lisa guessed he was going to check on the horses.

This is my chance, she told herself. *If Callie and I are going to be friends, I might as well start getting to know her a little better.*

She swam to the edge of the swimming hole and hoisted herself onto a wide, smooth rock that hung out over the water, wincing as her bare feet touched the sunbaked surface. Hurrying forward, she cooled her feet in the grass while she reached for her towel. She quickly squeezed most of the water out of her shoulder-length hair, then wrapped the towel around her waist.

Callie was staring intently at the grill when Lisa approached. "Hi," Lisa said.

Callie looked up. "Oh! Hi, Lisa. Having fun?"

"Sure." Lisa hesitated, uncertain what to say next.

Callie, too, was feeling at a loss for words. She swallowed, searching her mind for something intelligent to say. She had known that this moment had to come sooner or later, but she still wasn't prepared.

From her first week at Pine Hollow, Callie had recognized that Carole, Stevie, and Lisa were an especially close group. Best friends. It had made her feel awkward at first, like a third—or rather, fourth—wheel.

Then Lisa had gone off to spend the summer in California, and the accident had happened. As Callie had begun the slow process of recovery, she hadn't had much time to worry about who was friends with whom. She had simply accepted the help and companionship that Stevie and Carole, among others at Pine Hollow, had offered her. She had hardly been aware of it as their friendship gradually grew and deepened.

But she recognized it now. Callie had never met people like Carole and Stevie before. She had never had friends quite like them. And as the summer had progressed, she had come to feel more and more comfortable with them. But they had been Lisa's friends first, as Callie had suddenly remembered when the two of them had flown off to visit her in California. Somehow she had allowed herself to forget that, perhaps to forget that Lisa was ever coming home. But now she was here, and that threw the two of them into a weird, uncomfortable juxtaposition—both of them with the same friends but knowing next to nothing about each other.

Now Callie guessed that Lisa was feeling much the same way as she was herself. She felt some responsibility for reassuring Lisa, though she wasn't sure how to go about it. "This is great," she said, doing her best to sound cheerful and natural. "I used to go on trail rides back in my old hometown a lot. The trails were really spectacular there—mountains, canyons, the whole bit—but we didn't have our own private swimming pool in the woods like this." She gestured at the others, who were still splashing around in the swimming hole.

Lisa nodded. "You're from the West Coast, right?"

"Right. A little town at the foot of the mountains called Valley Vista." Callie bit her lip as a sudden wave of homesickness swept over her. "It's really beautiful there. I miss it a lot."

"That's only normal," Lisa said. "Still, it must be awfully exciting. Having a father who's a congressman, I mean."

Callie shrugged and poked at a half-cooked burger, sending up a plume of steam. "It can be, I guess. Scott—my brother—certainly seems to thrive on it. But it can sometimes make it kind of hard to make friends. Good friends, I mean—like you and Carole and Stevie are to each other." It wasn't easy for Callie to admit something like that to anyone, especially a virtual stranger like Lisa. But she wanted to make Lisa understand how things were—that she didn't have to worry, that Callie wasn't out to steal her best friends. If she'd had her choice, her family never would have moved to Virginia in the first place, so they wouldn't be having this conversation right now. But Congressman Forester thought it would be better to have his family with him full-time while he was on the job in Washington, so that had been that.

Lisa leaned over to pluck a stack of paper plates out of the grocery bag near the grill. "I guess it must be sort of like living in a fishbowl," she said. "Everybody watching your every move just because of your dad's job."

"Exactly." Callie smiled tentatively at the other girl. "Sometimes I wish he did something normal, like being a dentist or a computer programmer or a teacher or something. Then I wouldn't have had to leave my friends behind and move all the way across the country." Suddenly realizing that Lisa might think she was whining, she quickly added, "Not that it's been so terrible moving here."

"I understand." Lisa was carefully stacking the paper plates on a plaid picnic blanket someone had spread nearby. "You can't choose your family. Or control what they do."

At that, Callie remembered hearing that Lisa's parents had divorced a few years before. Fearing that she had unwittingly reminded Lisa of her own painful family problems, she did her best to shift the topic. "Anyway, Dad promised we could go back to Valley Vista for the holidays," she said. "I can't wait to hang out with the old gang." She shrugged. "Although actually, my friend Sheila e-mailed me a couple of days ago to say she might be coming to visit soon."

"Really?" Lisa asked. "That's a long way to go. You must be good friends."

"We've known each other for ages," Callie said, already wondering exactly why she had decided to bring up this particular topic. "Our mothers are best friends. But actually, the reason Sheila might be coming out here is that she's graduating this year from high school and is thinking about college."

"So, she's looking at schools here?" Lisa asked.

"Bingo." Callie flipped a burger that was starting to sizzle. "She's trying to talk her parents into making it a big trip. And if I know Sheila, she'll get her way. She's going to try to arrange it so that she can spend a few days with my family."

"That sounds nice," Lisa said, not quite certain how to respond. Judging by Callie's expression, she didn't seem exactly thrilled to be having this conversation with Lisa. Or was Lisa imagining that? Projecting her own discomfort onto the other girl? She did her best to smile normally as she continued. "I know it was really great when Carole and Stevie came to visit me in California. Not that it's the same kind of thing," she added quickly. "I mean, I was only out there for the summer. Not permanently."

"I know what you mean, though," Callie assured her. "You must have missed them a lot, even if you knew it wasn't permanent. Carole and Stevie are pretty special."

You don't have to tell me that Carole and Stevie are

special, Lisa thought. *I know them a whole lot better than you do. I've always known they're special.* She busied herself with digging another package of hamburger buns out of the bag, not wanting Callie to get a look at her face and suspect what she was thinking.

She felt guilty about her thoughts, knowing that Callie must be trying her best to make this awkward situation a little more comfortable. She wanted the same thing Lisa did—to ease this weird transition period so that they could all be friends.

Still, even though she knew it was stupid and petty, Lisa couldn't help resenting Callie's efforts. Suddenly feeling too confused by these swirling thoughts to try to carry on the conversation, Lisa dropped the bag of hamburger buns on the blanket and stood up.

"It looks like it's almost time to eat," she said as brightly as she could. "I'd better start rounding up the others."

Without waiting for Callie to reply, she turned and fled back to the safety of the water, leaving Callie alone at the grill.

SIX

"How's that, boy?" Carole murmured, rubbing a body brush firmly over Starlight's left shoulder blade. "Feels good to get that dust and sweat out of there, doesn't it?"

The horse couldn't answer, of course, at least not with words. But Carole understood the language of his grunts and sighs of pleasure and his half-closed eyes as easily as she would have understood it if he had said, "Wonderful, thank you."

She smiled and switched the brush to her other hand, moving slowly down his shoulder with short, firm strokes, working carefully, wanting to make his bay coat shine.

As much as Carole loved riding Starlight, she sometimes thought that these slow, leisurely groomings might be her very favorite part of owning a horse. Just the two of them, alone in a stall, oblivious to the rest of the world, resting their muscles after a day on the trail.

"Today was fun, wasn't it, boy?" Carole murmured, thinking back to their picnic. After gorging themselves on Callie's perfectly cooked burgers under the blazing midday sun, the friends had seriously considered breaking the rule they'd all had drilled into them since childhood by going right back into the water. Then Stevie had suggested an alternative: mounted games. They had all raced to get their horses ready, then spent the next hour playing shadow tag, running relay races, and generally goofing off like a bunch of D-level Pony Clubbers. By the time Carole decided it was time to stop and give the horses a rest, everyone was more than ready to jump back into the swimming hole and cool off. Even Callie had rolled up her jeans and waded—crutches and all—into the shallow area where the swimming hole joined the creek. After another hour or so of that, it was time to pack up the picnic supplies for the hour-long ride back home. Altogether, it had been the most fun and relaxing day Carole remembered having in ages.

But now that she was back in the stable, her thoughts were returning to business. She was getting more and more curious about exactly what Max had planned for her in the coming months.

She moved around to Starlight's right side and began working it over with the body brush. "Who do you think I'll get to train, huh, boy?" she whispered to the horse. "Firefly, of course. Ben and I are making pretty good progress with her, if I do say so myself. And then there's you. I never get tired of training you." She paused and ran over her mental list of Pine Hollow's equine residents, wondering which of the younger horses Max had in mind for further training. "Maybe that new pony he bought last spring," she murmured into Starlight's ear. The gelding's head was drooping contentedly as Carole ran her brush down his neck, and his eyes were still half closed. "Or maybe he wants me to help that new blond girl with that feisty little quarter horse of hers."

Starlight seemed to have no opinion on the matter. His head drooped even lower, and Carole suspected that he was all but asleep. She smiled and continued her grooming.

She was pleased with the way Starlight had performed that day in the mounted games. He had responded even better than usual to all her commands, making her realize just how far the two of them had really come in their training together over the years.

Maybe I was a little too hasty the other day, thinking that Starlight and I could never compete in a show like Colesford, Carole thought as her hands continued their task automatically. *Maybe we are good enough to compete with those high-class horses.*

Then she shook her head. They weren't quite good enough. Not yet. But maybe someday . . .

She wondered if Max had given any thought to entering one of his horses in the prestigious show. After all, it promised to be an important local event, and it would be good for business if a Pine Hollow horse competed and did well. Carole decided to mention it to him and offer to help if she could.

Feeling excited about the possibility of being involved in the Colesford show, no matter how marginally, Carole once again pulled up her mental list of Pine Hollow horses and riders. *Let's see,* she thought. *Who could handle that level of competition?*

A few names came to mind. Andrea Barry and her elegant hunter, Country Doctor. George Wheeler and his talented gray Trakehner mare, Joyride. Even Stevie and Belle might be able to hold their own in dressage if they worked extra hard between now and then, though they would be a long shot to win a ribbon.

She was pretty sure that she herself was good enough to ride in the show and not embarrass herself or Max, but she also knew that it would be difficult to work up a partnership with any horse other than Starlight in time, even if she wanted to.

Still, if Max wanted me to give it a try on Talisman, or maybe Topside, I probably wouldn't turn him down, she added to herself.

She gave Starlight a quick pat, startling him out of his doze long enough for him to open his eye and give her a slightly dirty look. "Sorry, boy," she said. "I'm just daydreaming. I would never want to work that hard with any horse but you. Besides, if Max asks anyone to ride for him, it'll probably be Denise. She's definitely ready for a top show like that. And she gets along great with Talisman. They'd make a fantastic team for the show."

Starlight's eye drifted shut again and he shifted his weight, letting out a contented snort. Carole fell back into her daydreams, this time picturing Denise McCaskill, Pine Hollow's stable manager and an accomplished rider, competing aboard one of Max's most talented show horses, the spunky and experienced chestnut gelding, Talisman.

They'll be perfect, she told herself happily. *They'll do Pine Hollow proud. And then maybe next year—* she gave Starlight another pat—*next year it'll be our turn.*

She returned her attention to her horse's grooming, carefully finishing his coat with the body brush and then stooping to retrieve a softer brush from her grooming bucket for his face.

A few minutes later, she was carefully sponging Starlight's eyes when she heard footsteps approaching in the aisle outside. Stepping back and stretching to work a kink out of her back, she glanced at the stall door, wondering who was out there. She'd thought her friends had all left the stable already, but maybe one of them was still around and was coming to say good-bye. Or maybe it was Ben. Carole hadn't seen him since their return, but she supposed he was lurking somewhere.

But when the footsteps stopped outside Starlight's stall and a head poked over, Carole saw that it was Max.

"There you are," he said.

Carole tossed the sponge she'd been using back into the grooming kit, picked up the bucket, and ducked under Starlight's lead line. As she approached the door, she saw that Max's face looked uncharacteristically thoughtful and somber.

"What's up?" Carole asked.

Max didn't answer for a moment. His blue eyes focused on Starlight, running up and down his body. "He looks good," he said finally. "You take good care of that horse, Carole. He's come a long way these past few years."

"Thanks." Carole was starting to feel puzzled and a little suspicious. Max looked so serious. But suddenly she didn't think it had anything to do with Prancer. Max would have spit that out right away. *Did I do something wrong?* she wondered. *Is he here to chew me out? Or is something else going on?* Her grip tightened nervously on the plastic handle of the grooming bucket as she tried to figure out what horrible mistake she might have made without realizing it.

Finally Max turned to meet her eye. "I have some news," he said. "Samson is coming home. Back to Pine Hollow."

Carole's breath caught in her throat. Her whole body suddenly seemed to go numb. The grooming bucket slipped out of her hand and crashed to the floor, spilling its contents over the stall's deep straw bedding.

SEVEN

"Samson?" Stevie repeated, pressing the phone's earpiece closer, wondering if she had misheard what Carole had just said. "Did you say Samson? *The* Samson?"

"That's right," Carole confirmed, sounding a little breathless. "He's finally coming home, where he belongs."

"But Max sold him to that trainer in the next county for his son to ride," Lisa protested. "That was almost three years ago, wasn't it?"

"That's right." Stevie nodded, though she knew her friends couldn't see her. Carole had called her a few minutes before and asked her to dial Lisa on the Lakes' three-way calling feature so that she could give them some important news. As soon as they were all on the line, she had announced that Max was bringing a horse named Samson to Pine Hollow. All three girls knew Samson very well. They had known both his parents and had assisted in his birth. But Samson had left Pine Hollow years earlier, and Stevie had thought of the coal black horse only occasionally since then. "I thought those two were destined to win every show-jumping ribbon in the universe or something," Stevie added, remembering that the horseman who had bought the young gelding had been thrilled with Samson's extraordinary jumping ability. Apparently the man's son, an accomplished rider in his early twenties who had dreams of someday making the Olympic equestrian team, had been searching far and wide for the perfect mount. Samson had been the answer to his prayers, and Max had sold the spirited gelding for a tidy profit.

Carole didn't give any indication of having heard Stevie's comment—or Lisa's, for that matter. She sighed on the other end of the line. "It's going to be so great," she said dreamily. "Samson back at Pine Hollow. Maybe Max will let me give him Delilah's old stall. Wouldn't that be perfect?"

Stevie held back her own sigh, twisting the phone cord around one finger. She was feeling a little impatient with Carole, but she was trying to hide it, since she knew her friend had always had a soft spot for this particular horse. Samson looked a lot like his sire, a fiery stallion named Cobalt that had died tragically after a riding accident. Carole had loved Cobalt more than any other horse before him, and she had taken his death hard. For a while, her grief had even made her consider giving up riding. Now that she thought about it, Stevie recalled that Carole had moped around for weeks after Max sold Samson, even though she had already owned Starlight for some time by that point. But eventually she had recovered from Samson's departure, too.

"This is like a dream come true," Carole went on, her words coming so fast that they tumbled over one another and Stevie could hardly understand her. "I couldn't believe it when Max told me. I thought I was hearing him wrong. But it's true. Samson. At Pine Hollow. Just like in the old days."

Stevie rolled her eyes. She wasn't really in the mood for this kind of good old-fashioned horse gossip, even with her best friends. She was feeling too distracted by other things—primarily Phil's new friendliness with Scott Forester. Upon their return to the stable that afternoon, the picnickers had found Scott waiting to give Callie a ride home. He had been as jovial as ever with the others, including Phil. But for Stevie he had only his usual cool stare and terse nod, even after she made a point of greeting him politely.

For the first couple of months after the accident, Stevie had assumed that she deserved every bit of disapprobation he sent her way. She had felt so guilty and so responsible for what had happened that she had accepted his behavior as understandable, even appropriate.

But lately, with help from her family and friends, including Callie, she had mostly moved past those feelings. She had finally started to believe that the accident had been exactly that—an accident.

That was why Stevie had vowed to change her attitude toward Scott, hoping it would help close the gap filled with bad feelings between them. But she had been doing her best, smiling and greeting Scott every time she saw him in the halls at school or the aisles of Pine Hollow, and Scott still was making no move toward reconciliation. That was starting to annoy Stevie—a lot.

What's Scott's problem, anyway? she thought, hardly hearing Carole's breathless reminiscences about Samson's first horse show a few years earlier, before Max had sold him. *I mean, Callie is getting better faster than anyone could have expected. She's riding again, and I'm sure she'll be back in training before we know it. She's already looking toward the future. Why can't her brother do the same thing and just get over it already?*

She tuned back in on the phone conversation, realizing that Lisa was speaking, sounding worried. ". . . and I thought that guy's son was serious about Samson."

"What?" Carole finally seemed to remember that

she wasn't just talking to herself. "Oh, yeah. They won a whole bunch of prizes already, even though Samson's pretty young. Remember? Max has all the clippings in his scrapbook in the office."

Stevie drummed her fingers on the bedspread, once again wishing Carole would just get on with it. "We know," she said with as much patience as she could muster. "We've all seen that stuff. That's exactly the point. If they were such a winning team, why's Samson coming back now?"

"Oh, I forgot I hadn't mentioned it," Carole said rather dismissively. "There was an accident."

Stevie's memory jolted. Unbidden, the image of Cobalt's long-ago accident ran through her mind, as clearly as if it had happened yesterday. They had all been in a jumping lesson, working on a cross-country course. Stevie had just jumped a fence on Comanche when she heard shouts and then hoofbeats behind her, coming much too fast. She had ridden Comanche off the course and wheeled him around just in time to see a classmate named Veronica diAngelo barreling down the hill on Cobalt, heading for the same fence Stevie had just cleared. The big Thoroughbred stallion's nostrils had flared, his long, slender legs pounding the earth at a full gallop as he followed his rider's deadly instructions.

Stevie had wanted to shout out for Veronica to stop, to slow down. At that speed there was no way

Cobalt could jump the high fence and land safely on the steep slope beyond. But it was already too late. Cobalt didn't slow down one bit. Stevie had held her breath and hoped with all her might that it would turn out all right. For a moment she'd thought she might get her wish. Cobalt had taken off, soaring over the fence as easily as most horses would have cleared an obstacle half its size.

But then he had landed. The impulsion of his big body, the force of gravity, the sheer weight of twelve hundred pounds of horseflesh were too much for his slender, fragile Thoroughbred forelegs. One of those forelegs had crumpled beneath him, and Cobalt had fallen forward, landing heavily on one shoulder as his rider flew off over his head.

Stevie had watched the whole scene as if it had been happening in slow motion, not even realizing she was crying and screaming at the same time until a few seconds later. In the end, the vet had determined that Cobalt's leg bone was shattered, and the gallant stallion had had to be destroyed. Veronica had been lucky and gotten away with only a broken arm—and the knowledge that she might have suffered much worse.

That whole terrible day flashed through Stevie's mind in an instant as she waited for Carole to go on. Had something similar happened to Samson?

Was he injured or lame? Was that why he was coming back to Pine Hollow?

By Lisa's simultaneous gasp of horror, Stevie guessed that she was thinking and wondering much the same thing. "Is he—Are his—Did he hurt himself? Samson, I mean?" Lisa asked.

"What?" Carole seemed momentarily confused by the question. "What do you—oh! No, I'm sorry. I should have been more clear. It wasn't a riding accident. Samson wasn't involved at all. He's fine. In fact, Max says he's in truly superior form. He's been training really well."

Lisa felt her pulse start to return to normal. She pushed her own nightmarish memories of Cobalt's death out of her mind. "Good," she said, waiting for Carole to go on.

But Carole seemed to have forgotten what she was talking about once again. "I was so excited that I forgot to ask Max exactly when Samson was arriving," she mused. "I'll have to ask him tomorrow. I guess it's probably too late to call now—I don't want to wake up the kids."

"Carole!" Stevie said sharply.

But once again, Carole didn't seem to hear her. "Max was lucky to be able to buy Samson back at the same price he got for him three years ago," she commented. "After all, he's had tons of training and conditioning since then."

Lisa took a deep breath, trying to focus her attention on Carole, who seemed to be getting more agitated and gleeful by the second. "Carole," she began.

But Carole's stream of words didn't abate. "It's really kind of a bargain for Pine Hollow when you think about it," she said eagerly. "He's already a prizewinning jumper, and I'm sure that with my help he can be even—"

"Carole!" This time there was no ignoring Stevie. Lisa winced a bit and held the phone away from her suddenly throbbing eardrum.

"What?" Carole sounded perplexed at Stevie's sharp tone.

Lisa could almost hear Stevie gathering every last scrap of patience. "You still haven't told us what happened," Stevie said. "The rest of the story. The accident. The reason Max is getting Samson back."

"Oh!" Carole sounded honestly surprised. "I didn't?"

"No," Lisa put in quickly, hoping to head off a full-fledged outburst from Stevie. "Please don't keep us in suspense any longer. Let's hear it."

"Well," Carole said thoughtfully, "I don't know all the details, but it was something like a boating accident. No, wait—scuba diving. That's right. Max said that guy—the rider, I mean, the one whose father bought Samson—was killed in some sort of scuba-diving mishap while he was on vacation a couple of weeks ago. Down in the Caribbean somewhere, I think."

Lisa gasped again, horrified—not only at the shocking tragedy of the young rider's death, but also at the appallingly offhand, almost casual way that Carole had just described it.

Once again, a hint of real concern crept into her mind as she remembered how deeply and irrationally Carole had loved Samson—and Cobalt before him. Lisa was starting to wonder if that irrationality had infected Carole again already. This just wasn't like the sensitive, kindhearted Carole that Lisa knew.

Then again, Lisa reminded herself, Carole often seemed to jump from one emotion to the next with hardly a pause in between, a pace that often left the more even-tempered Lisa dizzy. *She probably already sobbed her heart out for that poor young man before she called us,* Lisa thought uncertainly. *Now she's moved past that and is just excited about seeing Samson again.*

Maybe that excitement seemed a little overblown to Lisa, a bit exaggerated for a horse none of them had seen for years, but she wasn't at all sure it was her place to say so. They weren't kids anymore. Carole was older now than she'd been when Cobalt had died and when Samson had gone away. She was much more in control of her emotions than she had been back then. Besides, she had Starlight now. Things had changed. Things had changed a lot, actually, especially lately. . . .

Lisa sighed, her mind already wandering back to her problems with Callie, as Carole chattered on and on about Samson, hardly seeming to care whether or not her friends were listening.

EIGHT

"Here we are," Alex announced, braking in the Lakes' driveway. "Home safe and sound."

"No thanks to you." Stevie snorted. "If Mom and Dad ever saw the way you drive when they're not around, they'd rip up your driver's license and give the car to me."

"Whatever." Alex rolled his eyes and pulled the keys out of the ignition. "I thought you were only supposed to be this grumpy on Monday mornings. It's Tuesday, remember? And school's over for the day. Relax."

Stevie undid her seat belt and let herself out of the car without bothering to answer. She wasn't really feeling grumpy at all, and Alex knew it. In fact, she was in a good mood, mostly because she had decided during her study hall to call Phil when she got home and see if he wanted to get together sometime this week.

She whistled as she followed Alex into the house.

Taking the stairs two at a time, she went up to her room and shut the door behind her. Moments later, she was leaning back against her pillows, dialing the familiar phone number. After three rings, Phil answered.

"Hi there, sunshine," she sang out. "It's me."

"Hi, Stevie," Phil replied.

"Listen," Stevie said, "I had a great idea. You know that new CD store at the mall that everybody's been talking about lately? I was just thinking that we should check it out sometime soon, see if it's really all it's cracked up to be. Say, tomorrow after school?"

"Tomorrow?" Phil repeated. "Well, I don't know . . ."

"Come on," she urged. "What do you say? I'll come pick you up."

She smiled at the thought. It felt good to make that particular offer so casually, partly because she had been so conflicted about driving after the accident—actually, she had refused to drive at all for the better part of a month—but mostly just for the sheer freedom of finally being mobile, of not having to rely on other people for transportation. For one thing, it meant that her dates with Phil were no longer confined to weekends when their parents were free to chauffeur them around. Of course, Phil had earned his own license a couple of months before she had, but he didn't often have a vehicle at his disposal. His older sister, Barbara, had taken the family's extra car back to college with her at the end of the summer, and his parents were rather stingy about lending him their cars, at least in Stevie's opinion.

Suddenly she noticed that several seconds had passed and Phil hadn't responded to her suggestion. "Yo," she prompted. "Earth to Phil. Are you still there?"

"I'm sorry," Phil said quickly. "I guess I'm just a little distracted."

"What's up?" Stevie asked, suddenly realizing that Phil sounded kind of down. "Bad day at school?"

"You could say that." Phil let out a long, frustrated sigh. "It's A.J. He and Julianna broke up today."

Stevie gasped. "You're kidding!" she exclaimed. "What happened? They seemed as tight as ever on Saturday."

"I know." Phil sighed again. "And I have no idea what happened. A.J. won't talk to me about it."

Stevie raised one eyebrow. She was even more surprised by that than by the news of the breakup. A.J. had never been the type of guy to keep his feelings—good or bad—to himself. "Wow. I guess he's pretty upset, huh? Did Julianna dump him? I always suspected she'd break his heart one of these days. He's too trusting and happy-go-lucky."

"She didn't dump him," Phil corrected. "He dumped her. Right before lunch. I only know that because Julianna told me. She also told me he wasn't exactly tactful about it. Just walked up to her and told her it was over. No explanation, no nothing."

Stevie ran that through her head, trying to process it. She had never thought much of Julianna—she was nice enough, but a bit too giggly and girly for Stevie's taste—and she had always assumed that A.J. would come to his senses sooner or later and see that he deserved a girlfriend who had more to talk about than which shade of lipstick went with her dress. But whatever A.J.'s faults might be, he was a kind person, and a kind person didn't dump someone without any explanation.

"What could have happened?" Stevie said slowly, running all her memories of A.J. and Julianna from Saturday through her mind, looking for clues. But there weren't any. In fact, the couple had seemed more in love than ever—at lunchtime, they had spent more time kissing and tickling each other than eating. Stevie hadn't seen this coming. Not at all. From the tone of his voice, neither had Phil.

"He was out sick yesterday," Phil said. "I called him after school to see what was up, but there was no answer. I didn't really think much about it. Then at lunchtime today—Bam. Breakup city."

Stevie picked at a loose thread on her bedspread. "Do you think something happened on Monday?"

"I have no idea. All I know is that A.J. was acting weird all day today. I stopped by his locker before homeroom to see how he was doing, and he didn't have much to say. Just mumbled something about the twenty-four-hour flu and rushed away. I figured he still wasn't feeling great and let it go."

"Weird," Stevie murmured. She wasn't sure what else to say. It didn't make much sense. "Maybe he really was still kind of delirious," she offered. "Sometimes those flu symptoms can kind of bum you out for a while after you think you're over them."

"I thought of that," Phil admitted. "I'm hoping that's it. I guess we'll see. I'm going to give him a call a little later and see how he's doing. I just wish I knew what was going on with this Julianna thing."

"Don't worry," Stevie said, trying to reassure him. "A.J. is a good guy. And a good friend. He'll talk to you when he's ready. He probably just isn't handling this too well because Julianna was his first serious girlfriend."

"That's true." Phil sounded slightly mollified. "I hadn't really thought about it like that."

"It'll be fine," Stevie went on quickly. "You'll see."

Secretly she was starting to recover from her surprise enough to feel glad that A.J. and Julianna's relationship was over. Phil seemed to see it as some kind of tragedy, and Stevie sort of understood that. A.J. was his best friend, and if A.J. was hurting, Phil was hurting. Stevie felt sorry for A.J., too—and for Julianna, a little, though she suspected that it wouldn't take her long to bounce back—but she also thought that this was probably a good thing in the long run.

Maybe once he recovers we can try fixing him up with someone better, she thought. *He and Callie might be good for each other—he could help her lighten up, and she could bring out his smart and serious side. Or maybe we could even set him up with Carole, since she still refuses to admit that there's anything between her and Ben Marlow other than the pure and innocent love of horses.*

"I guess there's not much I can do except wait and see what happens," Phil said reluctantly.

"True," Stevie agreed. "A.J. will come to you soon enough. You'll see." Deciding it was time to take Phil's mind off his worries, she changed the subject to Samson. She had spoken to Phil on Saturday evening and mentioned that the horse would be returning to Pine Hollow, but the two of them hadn't talked since then. "He got there on Sunday morning," she said. "He looked as handsome as ever, though he's filled out a bit since we saw him last."

She pulled up a mental image of how Samson had looked stepping down off the ramp from the van that had brought him to Pine Hollow. He had paused and looked around, then let out a loud snort, as if he recognized the place.

Stevie's breath had caught in her throat as she and Lisa watched from their perch on the paddock fence.

"He looks just like Cobalt, doesn't he?" Lisa had whispered in awe.

Stevie had had to agree with that. The young horse was the spitting image of his sire, from the tips of his alert coal black ears to the high carriage of his long ebony tail.

Carole had been waiting to help Ben and Max bring Samson inside and bed him down in the stall she had made up for him. Stevie and Lisa had gone to offer their help, but Carole had shooed them away.

"I want to spend a little time getting reacquainted," she had told them, her wide brown eyes shining with anticipation and joy. "Max wants me to start working with him right away, so there's no time to lose."

Stevie told Phil the whole story now. "It turned out that Lisa and I were both a little worried about how Carole would react," she went on. "I mean, she spent most of Sunday getting Samson settled in, updating his file in the office, checking on him every two seconds. She even walked him around the stable yard for an entire hour because she wanted to make sure he hadn't gotten stiff on his trip over."

"Hmmm," Phil said. "Sounds like she's pretty excited to have him back. So why were you guys worried?"

Stevie hesitated, wondering how to explain. Phil had never known Cobalt—he and Stevie hadn't met until after that whole terrible time. "It's just that Carole always had a really special bond with Samson's sire. She took it really hard when he died. It almost made her give up riding. And now she seems so excited that Samson is back. . . ." She let her voice trail off, realizing that her concerns sounded silly when she said them out loud. Carole had been very vulnerable back then—not only because she had been so much younger, but also because it had all happened so soon after her mother had died of cancer. She was a different person now. Stronger, older, more mature, more focused, and more in control of her emotions and her life.

"I'm sure there's nothing to worry about," Phil said. "Carole gets excited any time Max gets a new horse. And you said she gets to train Samson, right? She must be thrilled. I remember what a fantastic jumper he was even before he left."

"True." Stevie shrugged, though she knew Phil couldn't see her.

She was starting to wonder what she had been so worked up about the day before. *I guess Lisa and I were probably a bad influence on each other,* she admitted to herself. *She tends to worry about anything and everything, and I suppose I can sometimes be a little bit quick to see excitement and intrigue in totally innocent situations. Not that I'd ever admit that to Phil!* She grinned at the thought. *He'd never let me live it down.*

"Anyway," she said, "Carole seems really happy so far. And you're right—training a superior horse like Samson can only help her become a better horsewoman. Max obviously thinks so, or he wouldn't have asked her to work with Samson." That last point settled her mind even more. Max was no fool. If he thought working with Samson would be any trouble for Carole, he wouldn't have decided to let her train him.

"Good point," Phil agreed. "I'm sure pairing them up will be good for them both. Has she started training him yet? I know he's only been there for about two and half days, but . . ."

"But you know Carole," Stevie finished with a

laugh. "And you're right. I stopped by yesterday after school for a quick ride and Carole was already at it when I got there. I stopped to watch them for a while."

"How did they look?"

"Well, you know how Carole's always been a pretty great trainer?" Stevie paused just long enough to lean over and pat the family dog, a big golden retriever named Bear, who had nosed open her bedroom door and lumbered in. "Well, now it seems that having a real star like Samson to work with has turned her into *Super*trainer. She never seems to lose patience with him. I think she could work with him twenty-four hours a day if she didn't think *he* needed some rest once in a while."

Phil chuckled halfheartedly. "That's great," he said.

Stevie guessed that he was still fretting about A.J. "I should probably let you go," she said, moving her legs to give Bear some space on the bed. "You're probably dying to get me off the phone so you can call A.J., right?"

"Never!" Phil protested so quickly that Stevie knew she had guessed right.

She laughed and scratched Bear behind one floppy ear. "Don't worry, I won't get jealous," she promised. "Go call him. You'll feel better once you two have talked."

NINE

Carole led Samson to the mounting block. "Steady, big fellow," she told him with a smile as she tugged on his lead to bring him a little closer alongside. "I'm not used to climbing way up on a tall horse like you."

She tucked her left foot into the stirrup and swung herself aboard easily. Despite her words, she knew very well that Samson was only about half a hand taller than Starlight. Still, she was sure that he looked at least seventeen or eighteen hands high. Maybe it was the aristocratic carriage of his neck and head, the long, slender, muscular legs that revealed the Thoroughbred blood of his sire. Or perhaps it was the elegant, flowing tail, so similar in everything but color to that of his beautiful palomino dam. Then again, it could have been the way his jet black coat glistened beneath the hot Virginia sun, seeming almost to be lit from within.

But Carole didn't really care about explanations

like that. All she cared about was that she was there, on Samson's back, with the whole afternoon stretching ahead of them.

She quickly leaned over to adjust her stirrups, shifting her balance in the saddle as Samson pranced energetically and tossed his head. "Ready to get started, fella?" she said, gathering up the reins.

She clucked to him and rode him toward the schooling ring, pausing just long enough to brush her fingertips over the battered old horseshoe—the lucky horseshoe, as it had been known to generations of riders at Pine Hollow—nailed to the stable wall.

"Not that I need any more luck," she murmured, leaning forward to give Samson a pat on the neck. "I'm already the luckiest girl in the world."

The horse let out a snort as if agreeing, and Carole laughed.

"Conceited," she accused him jokingly. Then she leaned over to open the gate, letting them into the ring.

She spent the next few minutes warming up, walking, trotting, and cantering, making sure the horse was relaxed and limber at each of the paces. Finally, when she was satisfied that he was ready to get to work, she brought him to a halt and sat back to think for a minute.

Max had told her a little bit about Samson's

training up to that point. The gelding had entered a number of show-jumping competitions with his previous owner, and Max had decided that Carole might as well continue conditioning him for that kind of event.

"A horse like Samson is never going to make a good schooling horse, anyway," Max had said, rubbing his chin thoughtfully as he and Carole watched the gelding eating his dinner on Sunday night.

Carole had nodded her agreement. She knew that some horses responded well to a variety of riders and some didn't. Samson needed a firm hand, but he was capable of a lot with the right rider.

"Are you thinking about showing Samson yourself?" Carole had asked Max.

He'd shrugged, his expression unreadable. "We'll see."

Thinking of the possibilities made Carole shiver. With Samson's talent, there was nothing he couldn't do, no show he couldn't enter.

"Maybe Max is thinking about Colesford," she whispered to the horse now, patting him once again. She hardly dared to think about that. It was just too exciting. In any case, it was time to get to work.

She had set up a small jump course in the ring before tacking up. It consisted of three medium fences set in a serpentine pattern. The obstacles weren't anywhere near as high as those Samson would be likely to encounter in a top-level competition, but Carole wasn't concerned about that. She knew Samson could clear just about anything. He could probably jump the stable roof if he really wanted to. She was more interested in making sure he would do as he was told, trusting his rider to guide him around the course without questioning it. In show jumping, the difference between a winning ride and an also-ran often came down to a time difference of a few seconds—or fractions of a second. Riders often had to make difficult decisions regarding speed, turns, and angles, doing their best to get their horses through the course quickly but cleanly.

Because it was only their second day working together, Carole was still taking it easy, simply trying to determine exactly what needed to be done. She took Samson through the course a few times, varying speed and direction. He jumped every fence with ease, seeming perfectly happy to do whatever she asked of him.

"Your last owner did good," she said, pulling up at one end of the ring and ruffling his mane. "You're just as wonderful as you used to be—maybe even more."

She smiled, thinking back to the old days, when Samson had been younger and less polished but had already shown signs of brilliance. When Lisa had ridden him in an important show in Pennsylvania, several members of the U.S. Olympic Team had been impressed with the performance—so much so that the girls had been afraid Max would sell him on the spot.

"Come on, big boy." She clucked and tugged lightly on the reins to get Samson's attention. "Time to get back to work."

Fifteen minutes later, Carole was riding Samson along the fence at a trot when she saw Ben approaching the ring from the stable building. She brought the horse to a walk and glanced over.

She bit her lip as he reached the fence and leaned his elbows on it, his eyes following Samson's every step. What was he doing there? She couldn't help feeling a bit self-conscious, as she often did when Ben watched her with that thoughtful, penetrating gaze of his.

"Oh, well," she whispered, more to herself than to the horse. "I guess I can't blame him for wanting to see your stuff, Samson. We'll just have to show him what you can do. Right?"

With that, she urged the horse back into a trot, then eased him smoothly into a canter as she brought him around to face the fences again. She put him through the course she had mapped out, then stopped him with a flourish just a few steps in front of Ben, who was still leaning on the fence, watching.

"Hi," she said, a little breathless from exertion, though Samson himself was hardly blowing at all. "What do you think of him?"

Ben let his eyes wander slowly from one end of the horse to the other before answering. "Nice," he said at last. "Good conformation. Good form over those fences, too."

Carole smiled, pleased. Coming from anyone else, Ben's terse words might have seemed like faint praise. But from him, she knew they were a glowing commendation. "Thanks," she said, fondly patting Samson's sweaty neck. "I don't know if Max told you, but he wants me to work with this guy from now on. He's a terrific jumper, and his sire was a Thoroughbred, so he's got a lot of natural speed, too. He already won a bunch of prizes as a show jumper." She realized she might be gushing, but she couldn't help it. She had to share her excitement with somebody, and Ben was right there, looking interested. "Max hasn't said so," she went on. "I mean, you know how he is, doesn't like to show his hand too soon. But he already said he didn't plan to use Samson as a school horse, so I bet he's planning to enter him in some shows, maybe as soon as this winter. I want to make sure he's as ready as he can be."

Ben nodded. "Sounds good. If you want, I could help you out with him. We could map out a detailed schedule to get him into top shape. Like the one we did for Firefly."

Carole hesitated. "Maybe," she said reluctantly. "But not right now. I think I need to spend more time alone with him first. You know—figure out where to go from here, what kind of schedule would work best for him."

If Ben was surprised at her response, he didn't let on. "Fine," he said, pushing away from the fence. "See you." He turned and walked quickly back toward the stable, disappearing inside a moment later.

Carole worriedly watched him go. "I hope he wasn't mad," she murmured. He hadn't looked or sounded angry, but sometimes it was hard to tell with Ben. Carole knew he could be sensitive, and the last thing she wanted to do was antagonize him—especially now that he was being a little more friendly again.

Maybe he's finally forgiven me for what happened this summer, she thought absently. But she wasn't really concentrating on Ben anymore. Her mind had already returned to her plans for Samson.

"Does your mom prefer plain instant rice or chicken-flavored rice supreme?" Alex asked, staring at the two boxes he was holding.

Lisa shrugged and pushed the shopping cart a little closer. "It doesn't matter," she said. "Get whichever one's cheaper. Mom hardly notices what she's eating these days anyway. I could feed her alfalfa pellets and she probably wouldn't notice."

Alex tossed one of the boxes into the cart and gave Lisa a sympathetic look. "I guess she didn't cheer up much over the summer, huh?" He turned to replace the rejected box on the shelf beside him.

"No." Lisa sighed. "I was hoping that having a couple of months to herself would give her time to think things through, maybe rediscover her own life and finally figure out how to move on." She shrugged. "Obviously I was wrong. She's just as bitter and angry as ever—though I think she was really happy to have me back home."

Alex reached over and squeezed her shoulder gently. "Well, I can't blame her for that. She's lucky to have you," he said. "For that matter, so am I."

Lisa smiled up at him. "Thanks," she said. "Now let's stop talking about my mother. This is supposed to be a date, right?"

Alex laughed and glanced around the supermarket aisle. A few yards ahead of them, a harried young mother was trying to soothe two yowling toddlers who were doing their best to fling food out of the cart as fast as she put it in. At the far end of the aisle, an elderly couple was arguing over the best brand of canned beans, while a supermarket employee tried to maneuver past them, pushing a cart piled high with rolls of paper towels.

"Some date," Lisa said ruefully. "Sorry to drag you along here. But I knew if I didn't get the shopping done today, Mom and I would be eating crackers and ketchup for dinner tonight." Since Mrs. Atwood no longer showed much interest in maintaining her now diminished household, Lisa was left with much of the responsibility for the shopping, cooking, and cleaning. Fortunately, Lisa had always been capable and responsible, and she managed to juggle these new duties without letting them infringe on her own life—not much, anyway. Sometimes, like now, she had to be a little bit creative to fit in everything she wanted and needed to do.

"I understand." Alex put one hand on the handle of the cart, helping Lisa steer around a stray toddler. "It doesn't matter. Anyplace we can be together seems like the most romantic place in the world to me. You know that."

Lisa just smiled at him again. She knew there was no need to put what she was thinking into words—Alex could read her complete agreement in her eyes. Maybe she wouldn't have chosen a crowded supermarket as the ideal spot for a date, but that didn't really matter. What mattered was that they were together.

That's what it's really all about, she told herself. *Being with the people you love.* She was thinking of Alex, but then her thoughts widened, unbidden, to include Carole and Stevie. And as soon as she thought of them, she remembered Callie. Callie, who always seemed to be around these days. Callie, who was now as much a part of life around Pine Hollow as Lisa herself. Maybe even more . . .

"What?" Alex had just looked at her face and noticed her frown. "What's the matter?"

"Oh, nothing." Lisa tried to laugh it off. But then she thought better of it. Maybe sharing some of her confusing thoughts and feelings about Callie with Alex would help her to sort them out in her own mind. "I was just thinking how friendly everyone has gotten with Callie these past few months."

"Yeah, I know," Alex agreed. "I have to admit, she seemed like kind of a snob at first. But she grows on you."

"Uh-huh." Lisa turned her face away, pretending to scan a shelf full of canned soups.

She should have known she couldn't fool Alex that easily. "What?" he demanded, reaching around to grab her gently by the chin. He turned her face back toward him. "Is something wrong? Is there some problem between you and Callie?"

"Not really." Lisa chewed on her lower lip, trying to figure out how to explain what she was feeling. "It's just that . . . well, it's weird, that's all. Coming home and seeing Callie so chummy with people. With Carole and Stevie, especially. It's kind of hard to get used to."

Alex shrugged. "That's only natural. But remember, she was here all summer. They had plenty of time to get to know her."

. . . *while you were away.* Lisa finished his sentence in her mind. Why did all their conversations these days seem to circle around to that fact?

Lisa shook her head. It was turning out to be a lot harder than she had expected to avoid this particular topic. "Never mind," she said quickly. "Callie and I will be friends before you know it." She searched for a way to change the subject before Alex started brooding over her time in California and the pleasant mood between them was ruined, or at least tainted. Suddenly she remembered a piece of news she hadn't shared with him yet. "So did I tell you about what happened when I stopped by Pine Hollow the other day?"

"You mean Sunday?" Alex shook his head. "You just said you went for a ride."

Lisa rolled the cart around the end of the aisle

and grabbed a bottle of sale-priced soda. "I did," she said. "I called ahead and Denise said no one else had signed up to ride Prancer that day."

She paused, still surprised at how unfamiliar those words sounded. There had been a time, not that long before, when she hadn't needed to reserve Prancer. When the mare had almost always been available to her whenever she wanted to go for a ride. When she had almost seemed like Lisa's own horse.

Times have changed, Lisa thought with a sigh.

Not wanting Alex to guess what she was thinking—like everything else these days, this change too could be traced directly to her summer away—she went on. "Anyhow, when I got there, Carole was riding Samson in the main ring," she said. "I stopped to watch, and when Carole saw me, she came over."

"How did Samson look?" Alex asked curiously.

Lisa smiled. Alex hadn't had the least bit of interest in horses or Pine Hollow back when Samson had been sold. But he had certainly heard enough about the big black horse over the years—living with Stevie, he had hardly been able to avoid that. "Samson looked great," Lisa told him. "We'll have to go over there soon so you can check him out. He looks even bigger and stronger than he did the last time I saw him, and he's still got all his old fire and spirit."

Alex nodded and pointed to a bin full of sponges. "Didn't you say you needed cleaning stuff?"

"Thanks." Lisa added a package of sponges to her cart. "Anyway, let me tell you about the weird part. When Carole heard why I was there, she got this really strange expression on her face."

"What kind of expression?"

Lisa shrugged. "You know Carole," she said, smiling fondly. "She's terrible at hiding her emotions, but she thinks she can keep people from guessing what she's thinking by tucking her lips into her mouth and raising her eyebrows. I think she thinks she looks innocent when she does that." She shrugged again. "So anyway, she gets that look on her face, and then she tries to convince me to take Firefly—you know, that new gray—out on the trail instead of Prancer."

"That's weird," Alex said. "Didn't she try to get you to ride her before?"

Lisa shook her head. "No. Last time she wanted me to ride Calypso," she corrected. "And I did, remember? But wait, there's more. I told Carole to forget it and went inside to get Prancer. I found Max sort of hovering around outside her stall. He started rambling on and on about Barq—how I used to ride him back before I started riding Prancer, how well we always got along together, what a great horse he is, that kind of thing."

"Weird," Alex said again. He kicked absently at the tire of the shopping cart as Lisa stopped in front of a display of breakfast cereals. "So what was that? Just an attack of nostalgia?"

Lisa sighed and bent down to retrieve a box of cornflakes from the bottom shelf. "Normally I would think so," she admitted. "But then when I made a move to start getting Prancer ready, he suddenly got all stern and told me I couldn't ride her that day. No reason, just said she was off-limits for a little while, then looked at his watch and took off before I could ask him anything about it."

"That is kind of strange," Alex admitted. "But Max can be kind of strange sometimes, you know. Anyway, what do you think is going on?"

Lisa shrugged and kicked at one wheel of the shopping cart, which was doing its best to roll crosswise to the other three. "Probably nothing," she admitted. "Max has been pretty busy lately, and I haven't been spending as much time at the stable as I used to, so I've barely seen him, let alone chatted with him about how Prancer is doing. For all I know she could be in the middle of some kind of special training program or something." She bit her lip, not wanting to sound paranoid or whiny. "Still, after what Carole said about riding Firefly . . ."

". . . you decided there was a conspiracy afoot," Alex finished for her. He chuckled. "Don't worry.

It's probably nothing, just like you said. Besides, I haven't been riding there that long, but even I know that Max is always encouraging people to ride as many different horses as possible. Maybe that's why he stopped by to chat about Barq and all the rest of it—because he thinks you need to branch out more. I mean, isn't he even making Carole ride Samson now, and Firefly, or whoever else it is she's supposed to be training? And she's got her own horse."

Lisa knew he was trying to help, but she didn't think much of his logic, and she said so. "Carole wants to work with horses professionally someday," she pointed out, heading slowly down the aisle again. "Of course she needs to get experience with as many different horses as she can." She shrugged. "But I mostly just ride for fun. And I have enough experience to know that I always have the most fun on Prancer."

"Hmmm." Alex looked thoughtful. "Good point."

Lisa smiled. One of the many qualities she loved in Alex was his ability to take criticism or contradiction without getting angry or defensive. He didn't have to be right all the time like so many of the other guys Lisa knew. It made him exceptionally easy to talk to, since she never had to censor what she was thinking. *Unless what I'm thinking about has anything to do with those two months in California,* a nagging little voice inside her added.

"Anyhow," she said, "I checked with Denise and she seemed kind of surprised. She didn't even know that Prancer was off-limits that day. So she wasn't really much help. She just told me that if I still wanted to go for a ride, Barq or Comanche or Checkers could use a workout. I took Barq out for a while, but it wasn't the same." She shrugged. "Still, if Denise doesn't know what's going on with Prancer, I guess it can't be too serious. I mean, she is the stable manager. Right?"

Alex shrugged and bent down to replace a fallen box on the shelf they were passing. "Who knows?" he said. "Why don't you just ask Carole if you're so worried about it?"

"I don't know." For the first time, Lisa realized that she really was being silly to worry. Sure, Max could sometimes be a bit abrupt or mysterious, but if there was anything going on with Prancer that she should know about, Carole would know. She spent almost as much time at the stable as the horses did, and she would have told Lisa immediately if anything was wrong with Prancer. They were best friends, weren't they? "Maybe your idea was right after all," she told Alex. "I've often suspected that Max wishes I would ride other horses sometimes, even though Prancer and I are so obviously perfect for each other."

"Maybe you should take his advice and experiment a little," Alex said. "I must have ridden five different horses since I started going there. It's fun to try out someone new once in a while."

"No way," Lisa replied quickly. "Didn't you hear me? I'm perfectly happy with Prancer. Trying to get me to ride other horses when I could ride her just doesn't make sense. It's like encouraging me to date other guys even though I already know I'm in love with you."

Alex looked a bit startled at the comparison. "I see your point," he said, obviously completely convinced. Then he changed the subject to the best kind of pickles, and that was the end of that.

10 TEN

A week later, Stevie and Callie were in the tack room at Pine Hollow. Stevie had just finished exercising Belle and was in the middle of a leisurely tack-cleaning session while she waited for Phil to arrive to pick her up for their dinner date. Callie had just finished her daily therapeutic riding session and had stopped in to chat.

". . . and it's amazing how much easier it all is since I started," Callie was saying. "The first time they put me on PC, I wasn't sure I'd be able to do it. It felt like he was doing all the work, and I was just sitting there like a big old sack of apples. But now . . ."

Stevie glanced up from the bucket at her feet and smiled. "I know," she said. "It's easy to tell how much better you're doing now just by watching you. I saw you trotting around the paddock on my way in just now, and if I didn't know better . . ." She let her voice trail off, not wanting to sound untactful. Callie already had to know that she looked a lot more, well, *normal* on horseback than she did when she had to rely on her own two feet — like now, for instance, as she supported part of her weight on a saddle rack and the rest on those ever-present crutches. She didn't need Stevie to remind her of that fact. To hide her thoughts, Stevie bent down and pulled the stirrup irons she'd been soaking out of the bucket, scratching one last bit of mud off one of the eyes with her fingernail. Then she looked up at Callie again. "Well, you know what I mean."

Callie nodded, a flicker of something—pain? annoyance? Stevie wasn't sure—passing over her face so quickly that it was gone almost before it registered. "Today was a good day," Callie said. "The kind of day that makes me think my doctors are right when they say I should be walking—and riding—perfectly normally soon." She paused. "Maybe by Thanksgiving," she added softly.

Even though Callie's words sounded cheerful, Stevie sensed an undercurrent of tension. "Are you okay?" she blurted out before she could stop herself. "Um, I mean, you look a little . . . I don't know . . ."

"I'm fine." Callie shrugged. "I told you. It was a good day." She hesitated, then went on. "Actually,

125

though, I guess maybe I'm a little distracted about something. In a good way, I mean."

"What is it?" Stevie stood to put away her stirrups. Then she walked over to the rack where Belle's sweaty saddle was waiting to be cleaned. "Did your parents decide to let you drop chem after all?" The two girls had spent quite a bit of time over the past week commiserating about their already perplexing assignments. Of course, Stevie hadn't bothered to share with Callie one reason she couldn't seem to concentrate in chemistry class—namely, that she spent far too much time glaring at Scott's impassive back in the front row when she should have been focusing on what the teacher was saying.

Callie let out a quick laugh. "No, no," she said. "Nothing quite that thrilling. But it's still really great news. I don't remember if I told you before, but my friend Sheila from back home has been talking about visiting me. And I just found out this morning that she's definitely coming. Soon."

"That's great!" Stevie unbuckled the girth from her saddle. "When does she get here?"

Callie had her eyes trained on Stevie's bridle. "That's still being worked out," she said. "She's stopping by as part of her Exclusive Universities of the East Coast tour, so she won't know until all her interviews are set up."

"Oh, she's a senior?"

"Yes," Callie said. "Sheila's always been really smart. She wanted me to try and finish high school in three years so we could go to the same college." She shrugged and smiled. "But once I got so into endurance riding I decided all that cramming wasn't for me after all. Sheila never let me live it down. Then again, I never let her live it down when she placed dead last at a horse show when we were both ten."

Stevie glanced up briefly from her work at the saddle rack. "Sounds like you two have quite a history."

"Oh, we do," Callie said quickly. "We've been friends forever. Our mothers were college roommates, and they had us playing together right after I was born."

"That's nice." Stevie scrubbed silently at a stirrup leather for a moment. She wasn't sure what it was, but something about Callie's expression still didn't seem quite right. Was her friend's upcoming visit really all that was on her mind? Somehow, Stevie wasn't convinced. Had something happened at her therapy session? At school that day? If Callie was upset or worried, Stevie wanted to help if she could. That was what friends were for.

Callie was still chattering on, describing the stable in California where she and Sheila had learned to ride together. Stevie watched her face carefully.

Yes, she was sure of it: There was a hint of something else behind that smile. Something worried, or maybe sad . . .

"Callie," she interrupted, "are you sure everything's all right?"

Callie frowned slightly. "I told you," she said. "I'm fine."

"Really?" Stevie persisted. "Because you know, if anything's bothering you, you can always talk to me. I—"

"Am I speaking English here?" Callie said sharply. "For the last time, I'm perfectly fine. Okay?"

"Okay. Sorry." Stevie turned her eyes back to her task, feeling properly chastised. She still wasn't convinced that Callie was telling her the whole truth, but it was clear she wasn't in the mood to share anything further with Stevie. It was at times like these that Stevie remembered that the two of them really had known each other for only a few months. Besides that, Callie was much more reserved and private than Stevie or her other friends. Stevie had to remember that—and respect it—if she wanted to hang out with her.

Fortunately, Callie's anger seemed to have passed as quickly as it had flared up. "So anyway, I've been meaning to ask," she said in a friendlier tone. "Have you heard anything new about A.J. and Julianna?"

Stevie smiled, grateful for the change of topic. She had filled in Callie—along with her other friends—about what Phil had told her the week before. "Not much," she reported, scrubbing at a grimy spot on her stirrup leather. "I talked to Phil last night. According to him, A.J.'s still keeping to himself about the breakup. In fact, Phil says A.J.'s hardly spoken to him—or to anyone else, for that matter—since it happened."

"I'm surprised." Callie lowered herself onto a nearby tack trunk, leaned her crutches against the end of it, and stretched her legs out in front of her. "I know I've only hung out with A.J. a few times, but he doesn't strike me as the strong, silent type."

Stevie smiled. "That's the understatement of the year," she said. "A.J. has been voted class clown every year since kindergarten. Mostly because he's always talking, telling jokes . . ." She trailed off, trying to reconcile the guy she was describing—the A.J. she had always known, the fun-loving person she had seen just a short while ago—with the sullen, withdrawn A.J. Phil had been telling her about for the past week.

Callie seemed to sense what she was thinking. "Don't worry," she said. "Like I said, I don't know A.J. anywhere near as well as you do. But I do know enough to have seen that he's a really levelheaded, smart guy. He'll come around." She shrugged. "I mean, you said Julianna was his first serious girl-friend, right? The end of a first relationship can be tough. Emotional, you know? Even if he's the one who ended it."

"That's what I keep telling Phil." Stevie sighed. "I guess he can't help worrying, though. Those two have been friends for a long time."

She was already starting to lose interest in the subject. She'd listened to Phil go on and on about A.J. for the better part of an hour the night before, and she'd said all she had to say then. She cared a lot about A.J., but she tended to agree with Callie on this one: He would come around when he was ready.

Callie reached for her crutches. "I guess I should get going," she said. "Scott should be here any minute to pick me up. I want to look in on PC before I go—he was so good today that I promised him a whole handful of carrots. And I still have to change." She swept a hand over herself to indicate the breeches and low boots she was wearing.

Stevie nodded. "See you tomorrow at school," she said. "Do you have another session tomorrow afternoon? I can give you a ride over here if you want."

"Thanks," Callie said, climbing to her feet. "I do have a session tomorrow. But are you coming straight here after last period? Because I want to get started as early as I can—my physical therapist wants me to take Friday off to rest my muscles, so I want to make sure I get a lot of work done tomorrow."

"Sure," Stevie assured her, smiling inwardly at the other girl's slightly anxious words. If there was one thing Stevie had learned about Callie, it was that she always worked hard at anything she cared about. And she definitely cared a lot about riding, not to mention getting back the full use of her body. "I'll have you here as fast as the speed limit allows." Suddenly something occurred to her. "Hey, does this mean you're free on Friday afternoon?"

"Like a bird," Callie said, not looking entirely pleased at that fact.

"Good," Stevie said. "Lisa and I were talking about getting together for a nice long trail ride. Why don't you come along?" She grinned mischievously. "I won't tell your therapist if you don't."

Callie smiled. "That sounds great," she said. "I'll be there—if you're willing to give me a ride over here two days in a row."

"Deal," Stevie said promptly. She had been working steadily as they talked, and now she realized that her tack was almost clean and Phil still hadn't shown up. She glanced at her watch.

Callie noticed. "Got an appointment?"

"Yes," Stevie replied. "And he's late."

"So am I. I'd better go before Scott has my hide." Callie gave Stevie a little wave and headed out of the room.

Stevie quickly gave her saddle a few final swipes, then returned it to its usual spot. She brushed off her hands, taking one last deep breath of the pungent leather-and-soap-scented air of the tack room before heading for the door herself.

"Okay, Phil, what's the holdup?" she muttered as she hurried down the hall.

She spotted the answer as soon as she rounded the corner. Phil was leaning against the wall near the main door, one sneakered foot propped against the wall behind him, a big smile on his face, looking incredibly cute in his favorite well-worn Washington Redskins jersey and faded jeans. He was deep in conversation with someone, and Stevie's eyes widened involuntarily as she recognized that someone. It was Scott Forester.

She stopped short, taken by surprise, not sure whether to interrupt them. Neither of them had noticed her. They were too busy talking and laughing. *Here we go again,* she thought, a bit disgruntled.

She knew that Scott liked to talk, and that he could strike up a conversation with just about anyone. But why did he have to choose her boyfriend so often?

She took a cautious step forward, then another,

feeling decidedly awkward. Finally, as she came within a few yards of them, the boys noticed her. Phil smiled in greeting. Scott looked up, and his own smile froze and faded from his handsome, open face.

"I'd better go find Callie," he mumbled, his voice suddenly subdued. "See you." He gave a wave that might or might not have been meant to include Stevie. A moment later he was gone.

Stevie joined Phil by the door and tipped her head back for a kiss. Then she glanced in the direction Scott had gone. "So," she said, trying to sound casual. "You guys looked like you had a pretty lively little chat going there."

Phil shrugged. "Whatever," he said, rubbing one hand over his shirt. "Guess what? Scott just offered me an extra ticket to the Redskins game on Sunday. Isn't that cool?"

"Huh?" Stevie wrinkled her forehead, not sure she had heard him right.

"It was supposed to be some kind of father-and-son outing, but his dad just agreed to head up some congressional commission or other, so he's got to work that day."

"And Scott invited you?" Stevie laughed uncertainly. "What, doesn't he have any other friends?"

Phil shrugged again. "I guess he figured I'd appreciate it. You know, because of this." He tugged on his jersey. "Anyway, what's the big deal? You seem kind of mad."

Stevie took a deep breath. She wasn't mad—not exactly. Just confused. Maybe a little annoyed . . . "I guess I just didn't realize you two were such good buddies," she said evenly.

"You know me." Phil laughed. "Anyone who likes the Skins is my buddy." He took her by the arm and gave her a searching look. "Hey, you're not upset because of—you know—you and Scott, are you? I thought we talked about that the other day and you were cool with it."

Stevie tried to turn her face away from him. "Of course I'm not upset," she muttered. "What do I have to be upset about? This has nothing to do with me."

"Don't give me that." Phil grabbed her dark blond ponytail with his free hand and gave it a gentle yank. "I know you, Stevie Lake," he said teasingly. "You're upset because you think Scott's stealing me away from you and you won't have anyone to boss around anymore."

Stevie couldn't help smiling. Phil really knew how to get to her. And after all their years together, he often seemed to know what she was thinking before she knew herself—especially if it was something dumb or illogical, like this. "Don't be ridiculous," she snapped, mostly joking now herself. "You and Scott would make a terrible couple. I mean, who would wear the gown when it was time for the prom?"

Phil pretended to look thoughtful for a moment, then grinned. "You're right," he said, putting both arms around her and squeezing so tight he lifted her right off the floor. "You'd look much cuter than he would in a tux."

Stevie laughed out loud this time. Then she gave him a kick in the shin. "Put me down," she ordered.

"Not until you say I can go to the game with Scott," Phil wheedled in a little-boy voice.

"Fine. Do whatever you want. See if I care," Stevie said, but her words didn't have much bite to them now. As Phil lowered her to the floor and released her, she shrugged. "Who knows? Maybe you can even put in a good word for me at half time. You know, explain to him that I'm really not second cousin to the devil."

"I thought it was first cousin." Phil ducked to avoid her swinging fist, then went on. "And it's a deal. I'll talk you up so much, Scott will probably want to invite *you* to the prom by the time the game is over."

"Fat chance," Stevie said. "Come on. Let's get out of here."

She led the way to the locker room, where she

had left her backpack. She felt a little better now about Phil's new friendship with Scott, but still not good. As stupid as she tried to convince herself it was, she still felt bothered by the idea that Phil would want to hang out with someone who had made her life so miserable these past months. He knew how upsetting Scott's coldness was to her—she had told him often enough.

Still, she decided as she grabbed her black nylon backpack, it wasn't worth getting into a fight over. It was just a football game.

She and Phil didn't run into Scott or Callie as they left the stable. But once outside, they did spot another familiar face in the schooling ring.

"Look, there's Carole," Phil commented. "I didn't see her on my way in."

Stevie frowned. "I didn't even know she was here," she said, although as soon as the words left her mouth she realized how silly they were. Carole was *always* there. She hardly left the stable except to sleep, eat, and go to school. And she did the last two under protest. But a second later Stevie realized why she had jumped to the unlikely conclusion that her friend had skipped a day. "I noticed that Starlight looked a little frisky and restless when I walked by his stall earlier," she explained.

Phil wasn't paying much attention. His eyes were following Carole and her mount as they cantered smoothly in a wide circle and then turned toward a row of cavalletti lined up on the ground in the center of the ring. Samson didn't hesitate as he reached the cavalletti and shifted into a trot to negotiate them. "Samson is really something, isn't he?"

Stevie nodded. "Let's go say hi."

She and Phil were almost to the fence when Carole brought Samson around again at the end of the course and spotted them.

"Hi!" Carole called. "I didn't know you guys were here."

Stevie waited for her to trot over to the fence before she answered. "I was just going to say the same thing to you." She couldn't help smiling when she got a good look at Carole. Her hard hat was slightly askew, several dark curls had twisted their way out from underneath, and dirt was caked on one cheek. But Samson's dark coat was spotless, aside from a bit of dust he had kicked up in the ring. That was typical. Carole never paid much attention to little details like personal grooming when she was wrapped up in her work at the stable, but the horses she cared for always looked flawless. "When did you get here?"

"Right after school." Carole leaned forward and patted Samson. "We were in the indoor ring for a while, but when I saw that Callie's session was finished, I decided we might as well take advantage of the nice weather and move out here."

Phil reached out to rub Samson's dark nose. "He's looking good, Carole. The fresh air must agree with him."

Stevie grinned. "I bet it would agree with poor Starlight, too," she quipped. "He just told me he's been cooped up in his stall so long he forgot what sunlight feels like."

"Don't worry about him," Carole said quickly. "Samson and I were just finishing up. I'm going to tack up Starlight right away and give him a nice long workout."

"Good. See you." Stevie turned away, her mind already returning—despite her best intentions—to worrying about Phil's new friend, Scott Forester.

ELEVEN

Lisa was humming as she left school on Friday afternoon. It had been a good day—her Spanish class had gotten their first quiz grades back, and Lisa had scored an A+. *"Perfecto,"* she whispered to herself as she unlocked the door of her car in the student parking lot, relishing the memory of her teacher's comment. She smiled as she slid behind the wheel, only wincing slightly as her hand touched the hot vinyl seat. So far her senior year was off to a great start, academically at least.

She was still humming a few minutes later as she spun her steering wheel expertly, swinging her car into Pine Hollow's gravel driveway. Now that the school week was over, she was really looking forward to today's trail ride. She had barely seen Carole all week, aside from the occasional greeting in the halls. Because they were a year apart, they ate lunch at different times and had no classes together. And she hadn't seen Stevie at all, although she had talked to her on the phone to plan this get-together.

She parked in the shade and jumped out of the car eagerly. As she turned to lock the door—completely unnecessary at bucolic and crime-free Pine Hollow, but a habit drummed into her during her summer in southern California—she heard the sound of another car crunching toward her over the gravel. She looked up, squinting against the glare bouncing off the chrome fender but immediately recognizing the dark blue two-door that Stevie and Alex shared.

Lisa stopped whistling when she noticed that Stevie wasn't alone in the car. Callie was sitting in the passenger seat, tying her blond hair into a ponytail as she laughed at whatever Stevie was saying. *What's she doing here?* Lisa wondered, her stomach clenching involuntarily.

Then she relaxed. Callie and Stevie went to school together. Stevie was just giving her a ride here. Why should she let something like that bother her?

She did her best to smile sincerely as the two of them climbed out of the car. They didn't notice her at first.

". . . so that's when kids started calling her Ms. Smoochie behind her back. It stuck even after she and Mr. Wensleydale stopped dating."

Callie was practically doubled over with laughter. "No wonder everyone snickered when she told us on the first day not to bother to 'kiss up' to improve our grades."

"Believe me, ever since then Miss Fenton has frowned upon letting teacher couples chaperone the—Oh, hi, Lisa," Stevie said, interrupting herself.

Lisa greeted them both politely. Then she turned to Stevie. "Ready for our trail ride?"

"Sure," Stevie replied cheerfully. "Oh! I hope you don't mind. I invited Callie along, okay?"

Lisa did her best not to let the sharp stab of disappointment she was feeling show on her face. "Great," she said with as much false cheeriness as she could muster. It was no big deal. It was just a trail ride. Why shouldn't Callie come along if she wanted to? "Let's go get tacked up, then. Is Carole here yet?"

Lisa forced herself to make small talk with the other two girls as they entered the stable building. Then she excused herself as the others turned toward the tack room.

"I want to give Prancer a quick grooming first," she told them. "It won't take long—I promise."

She felt herself relaxing again as she hurried down the aisle toward Prancer's stall. It was silly to be so uptight about Callie's presence. It wasn't as though this was some kind of Saddle Club reunion trail ride or anything like that. It was just a few good friends getting together for a relaxing excursion. And wasn't Callie a good friend?

Stevie and Carole certainly seem to think so. The little voice in her head piped up before she could squash it. Lisa shook her head. She would feel better when she felt Prancer's soft nose shoving at her neck, looking for treats.

She picked up the pace, eager to greet the loving mare. But when she reached the stall and peered inside, she found an unpleasant surprise waiting for her. Prancer was nowhere in sight.

"Prancer?" Lisa said, feeling slightly foolish. It wasn't as though Prancer was going to leap out of a dark corner at her call. The stall was empty.

Lisa glanced around the aisle helplessly. Hadn't she told Max she would be going on a trail ride this afternoon? She thought back carefully. Yes, she was sure of it. In her usual organized manner, she had called and left a message on the answering machine at the stable office as soon as she had gotten off the phone with Stevie. So where was Prancer? It had been almost a week since the day Max had told her the mare was off-limits, so it couldn't still have something to do with that, could it?

Maybe he never got the message, she told herself

uncertainly. Then she thought of another possibility. *Or maybe Prancer is on her way back right now.*

That made her feel a little better. Prancer had become very popular with the junior-high Pony Clubbers while Lisa was away. And those younger riders didn't always have the clearest grasp of the concept of time. Maybe someone had taken her out right after school and was just running a little late in getting her back for her scheduled ride with Lisa.

That must be it, Lisa reassured herself. *I just hope she's not too tired for another ride. I may have to keep it to a walk today . . .*

At that moment she heard footsteps approaching, and a second later Ben came into view around the corner, a halter slung over one broad shoulder and a grooming bucket in his hand. He glanced at Lisa and gave her a brief nod of greeting.

"Hi, Ben," Lisa said, putting out a hand to stop him as he started to hurry past. "Listen, do you know where Prancer is? I mean, did one of the younger kids take her out?"

"Nope," Ben said.

Lisa frowned. She wasn't in the mood to deal with Ben's taciturn habits. "Well, where is she, then?" she asked rather testily.

Ben didn't seem to notice. "Judy's got her out back."

"Judy?" Lisa repeated, feeling her stomach clench

with worry. Judy Barker was the local equine vet. "Is anything wrong?"

Ben shrugged again. "I wouldn't know about that. You'd have to ask Max."

Lisa's mind was working overtime to process this new bit of information. Why would Judy have taken Prancer out of her stall? Suddenly all her vague suspicions and vaguer worries of the past few weeks focused on that one fact. "There's not something wrong with her weak foot again, is there? I mean, did she go lame or—"

"I told you," Ben muttered, ducking his head. "You'll have to talk to Max. All I know is I saw Judy leading her down the aisle a few minutes ago."

He started to turn away, but Lisa grabbed him by the sleeve. He stared down at her hand for a second, looking surprised and slightly disturbed at the contact. "What is it?" he growled.

Lisa ignored his expression. She couldn't worry about Ben's famous gruffness right then. She wanted to explain to him how worried she was—how much she loved Prancer. How she was terrified at the very possibility that something could be wrong with her, wrong enough for Judy to come. Instead, her mouth formed completely different words. "But I was supposed to ride her today," she said blankly. "I called ahead."

Ben shrugged. "Things happen."

Lisa couldn't help noticing that he didn't seem terribly sympathetic. *I don't know why Carole cares if this guy is her friend or not,* she thought with a flash of anger. *I mean, he's pretty cute, but he could definitely use a personality transplant!*

She immediately felt guilty at the uncharitable thought. Ben's heart was in the right place, and he was wonderful with horses. She knew that. He just needed a little work on his people skills.

Lisa took a deep breath, forcing herself to remain patient. If she wanted Ben to help her out, she couldn't start yelling at him. That wouldn't do either of them any good. Ben would probably just walk away, and Lisa would be left feeling guiltier than ever—and no closer to any answers about Prancer. "Okay," she said evenly. "I guess we have a bit of a problem here. I'm supposed to be leaving on a trail ride right now, and I called ahead to reserve Prancer. What do you think I should do?"

Ben shrugged again. "Ride another horse." He clearly thought the answer was obvious.

Lisa gritted her teeth, feeling her annoyance swelling again. He had totally missed the point. Of course she could ride another horse if she had to. *Goodness knows, I've done that often enough recently,* she thought. But first she needed to find out what was going on with Prancer. And she needed to find out immediately, before she left on her trail ride, before she drove herself crazy with worry. As she was trying to pull her thoughts together so that she could start explaining that to him, she heard a voice calling her name from the end of the aisle.

"There you are!" Carole said breathlessly, hurrying over. She shot Ben a glance and a smile. Ben nodded in response, then slunk off.

Lisa wasn't sorry to see him go. "Do you have any idea what's going on with Prancer?" she demanded, stepping toward her friend. "Ben just told me Judy took her out, but he wouldn't say anything else. I'm afraid she must have hurt that pedal bone again . . ." Without waiting for a response, she turned and started down the aisle. Judy and Prancer were probably out in the back paddock, or maybe in the indoor ring. There was nothing to do but track them down and find out what was going on.

"Wait!" Carole raced after her, breaking Max's strict rule about running in the stable. She caught her by the arm. "Um, you probably shouldn't bother them. Judy is busy, and—well, besides, you don't have to worry. Prancer's fine."

Lisa stopped and turned to look at her, hardly daring to believe her ears. Relief washed over her, so strong her knees went weak. "Are you sure?" she said. "What's going on?"

Carole blinked quickly a few times, then glanced from side to side as if searching for an escape route. Lisa had seen that look before. Suddenly suspicious again, she crossed her arms and waited, sure that her friend's natural loyalty and honesty would win out.

"Nothing's going on," Carole assured her, finally meeting her eye. "Judy stopped by to check on Romeo's abscess, and she decided to take Prancer out for a quick ride. She is her co-owner, you know."

"Oh." That stopped Lisa short. She had completely forgotten that the vet and Max had bought Prancer as partners. Suddenly her wild worry and panic fled as quickly as they had come, until she felt like a deflated balloon. "I guess that means I'll have to ride someone else today. Again," she said dully.

"I guess so," Carole said brightly. "And I have a great idea. Why don't you give Eve a try? She hasn't been exercised yet today, and she's really sweet. Plus her trot is to die for—smooth as molasses but six times as fast."

For a second Lisa felt stubborn and opened her mouth to protest. She wanted to ride Prancer, not Eve, and if she couldn't ride the horse she loved, she didn't feel like going on a trail ride at all. But she snapped her mouth shut quickly, realizing how childish she was being. *It's no big deal,* she told herself. *I'm a mature human being. I can ride a different horse for one day—or rather, one more day—and still have fun.*

"Okay," she said, forcing the word from her mouth. "Can you show me which tack is hers?"

Carole nodded eagerly and headed in the direction of the tack room, chattering away about Eve.

Lisa bit back a sigh as they walked down the aisle past Prancer's empty stall. She knew that Carole was trying to make her feel better, and she knew that Eve was a very nice horse. She also suspected that she herself was overreacting a little.

I can't help it, though, she thought glumly, suddenly catching the faint sound of laughter coming from PC's stall, which was close to Belle's. *It's just one more sign that things aren't the way they used to be around here.*

Carole wiggled her elbow to dislodge a pesky fly. Starlight cast his ears back toward her for a second, but then, apparently deciding that she wasn't trying to tell him anything by wiggling his reins like that, he returned his attention to the trail.

Carole smiled and patted him, making him flick his ears toward her again. Then she sat back in the saddle and glanced forward to see how Lisa was doing.

She and Eve really seem to like each other, she

thought hopefully, noticing the relaxed looseness of the gray mare's stride. *I just wish I could tell her the real reason . . .*

She sighed. Max's secret was weighing more heavily on her with every passing day, and right then it filled her mind and made it difficult to relax and enjoy this trail ride with her friends. Behind her, she could hear Stevie and Callie trading quips and laughing easily. She only wished her guilty conscience would leave her alone so that she could join in.

I hate this, she thought unhappily. *Poor Lisa still has no idea, and I don't know how much longer we can keep fooling her like this. She deserves to know the truth—but I can't tell her. If it were anyone but Max . . . But I just can't. If he found out I'd spilled the beans, he'd never trust me again.*

She knew she couldn't risk that. She took her responsibility to Max very seriously. He had contributed more than any other single person in her life to her riding education. She owed him.

Besides, he might get so mad he'd decide not to let me train Samson anymore, Carole reminded herself, shuddering at the thought. *Anyway, Lisa will find out soon enough, whether I tell her or not. Then she'll be so excited that she won't even remember these little disappointments.*

Her conscience mollified a bit, Carole tried to

forget about secrets and go back to thinking about Samson. She had been pleased with his progress that week—so pleased that she was giving him a day off to graze in the paddock while she was on this trail ride. Still, she figured that if they got back early enough, there might be time to longe him for a few minutes before she had to head home for dinner.

That's a great idea, she told herself. *A little longeing would probably do him a lot of good.*

Looking forward to carrying out her new plan, she signaled for Starlight to lengthen his stride a bit. "Hey, you guys," she called out. "How about we trot for a while?"

TWELVE

Stevie drummed her fingers on her desk. Her chemistry teacher was droning on and on about the periodic table of the elements and all sorts of other things that Stevie was sure were going to turn up on the next test, but she just couldn't concentrate on any of it.

Why do we have to go to school on Mondays, anyway? she thought irritably. She glanced through the wavy glass of the classroom's old-fashioned bay window to the sunny afternoon sky. *Especially gorgeous, perfect, sunny, summerlike Mondays like this one.*

It was a familiar thought—Stevie had entertained some version of it for each of the last eleven Septembers of her life—but today it wasn't holding her full attention any more than Ms. Rourke's lecture about cadmium and selenium and who knew what else. She was distracted by nagging thoughts about Phil—more specifically, her phone conversation with Phil the evening before.

151

I still can't believe he had such a great time at that stupid football game yesterday, she thought. *But I guess he must have. Heaven knows he couldn't stop talking about it for more than two seconds at a time.*

Her gaze wandered to a certain broad, polo-shirt-covered back in the front row of the classroom. She still found the idea that her boyfriend could be friends with Scott Forester more than a little irritating. When she thought about it rationally, she knew she shouldn't feel threatened or angry or peevish about it. But Stevie wasn't always good at looking at things rationally. All she knew for sure was that she wished that Phil had decided not to go to that Redskins game—that he and Scott had never had that first friendly chat in the locker room at Pine Hollow.

Or better yet, Stevie added, *that Scott had never moved here in the first place.*

She immediately took back that wish. If Scott's family hadn't moved there, she would never have met Callie. And despite the accident and all the heartache it had caused Stevie and other people, she couldn't honestly wish for that.

Besides, last night after hanging up with Phil, Stevie had convinced herself—almost, anyway—to cut him some slack and not worry too much about the whole Scott thing. For starters, Scott seemed to have some kind of hereditary politician's compulsion to befriend everyone he met. He would probably forget all about Phil soon and move on to someone else. As for Phil, he would almost certainly be less interested in hanging out with Scott once A.J. returned to normal.

Stevie sighed and leaned her chin on one hand, propping her elbow on her desk. Ms. Rourke had moved on to a description of an upcoming lab assignment, and Stevie knew she should probably try to pay attention. But there were just too many other things to think about.

Her mind wandered back to A.J. On the phone, Phil had expressed as much concern as ever about his friend's increasingly odd behavior.

"He hardly talks to me anymore," he'd told Stevie. "Sometimes when I say hi in the halls at school, he just looks through me like I'm not even there. And it's not just me. He treats all his friends the same way."

Stevie had made her usual sympathetic noises, but that hadn't appeared to comfort Phil very much.

"This just isn't like him." His voice had been subdued and puzzled, as it always seemed to be lately when discussing this particular topic. "I tried to call him this morning before I left for the game, and his mom said he'd left the house hours ago. She had no idea where he was." He'd paused and let out a noisy sigh. "He's like a totally different person, Stevie. You haven't seen him since that day at the creek. You wouldn't recognize him now."

"He's just upset about what happened with Julianna," Stevie had said for about the hundredth time since this whole thing had started.

"I just don't get it," Phil had replied. "I mean, okay, if *she'd* dumped *him* I could maybe understand it. But he broke up with her. And she claims she has no idea why. She's just as mystified as the rest of us—and upset, too. She thought things were going great between them. It just doesn't make sense."

"It'll be okay. You'll see." Stevie's words had sounded a little lame, even to her. But she didn't know what else to say. They would just have to wait for A.J. to come around. And he would come around, sooner or later—Stevie was sure of it. In fact, at this point she really wasn't sure there was anything Phil should be getting so worked up about. Secretly she couldn't help wondering if maybe he wasn't exaggerating A.J.'s behavior just a teeny bit. It had to hurt when your best friend didn't feel like discussing his life with you—Stevie had encountered the same kind of feeling herself. But it would work itself out eventually. These things always did.

Suddenly Stevie popped out of her reverie as she

became aware that someone was calling her name. She had almost forgotten where she was. Now she realized that her teacher was staring at her.

"Stevie Lake," Ms. Rourke said again.

"Sorry!" Stevie sputtered. "Um, present?"

The class tittered. Stevie felt her face grow pink.

"Sorry," she said again, sounding as sincere as she knew how. "I—I was just thinking about what you were telling us before. You know, about the periodic table?"

Ms. Rourke pushed her red-tinted glasses farther up her nose and glared at her. "All right," the teacher said in her high, quavery voice. "Since you're so fascinated by the periodic table, I'm sure you'll truly enjoy this lab. Now, would you please go join Sue at lab table number four?"

Stevie smiled sheepishly as she realized that several of the other students had moved out of their seats and gone to the lab area at the back of the room. *I guess I must have been more out of it than usual,* she thought, sliding out of her chair and hurrying to the back of the room. She gave Sue Berry, who was already perched on one of the stools at table number four, a quick smile. Sue, a smart, quiet girl who had transferred to Fenton Hall a couple of years earlier, smiled back shyly. Stevie hopped onto the stool on Sue's right.

Meanwhile, Ms. Rourke was consulting the list in

her hand. "All right," she said dryly. "Now that Stevie is with us again, let's continue. The third member of lab group number four"—she pushed her glasses up again and squinted—"is Scott Forester. Scott, will you take your place at table number four, please?"

"Sure thing," Scott replied equably, pushing himself out of his seat and loping toward the lab area. His usual expression of amiable friendliness was intact, but Stevie noticed that he didn't quite look at her as he took his seat on the stool to Sue's left.

Stevie felt her heart sink. Of all the rotten luck! As if it weren't hard enough going to the same school as Scott and being in the same class, now they were actually expected to be lab partners?

". . . and Dad won by a landslide, so here we are! I miss Valley Vista, of course, but the people here in Willow Creek are so friendly and nice we haven't had any trouble at all feeling right at home. And Dad loves the short commute to Congress."

Stevie rolled her eyes and did her best to hold back a disgusted snort. Scott had been talking Sue's ear off ever since Ms. Rourke had finished assigning the lab groups and left the students alone while she went to fetch something from the supply closet down the hall.

"Don't you have a sister who goes here, too?" Sue asked Scott timidly. She seemed a little awed by him, and Stevie couldn't really blame her. Scott could talk the stripes off a zebra if he really tried. "I think she's in my English class. Cassie?"

"Callie," Scott replied with a dazzling smile that made the correction seem like a compliment. "She's a junior. I'm actually a senior, but contrary to popular belief, I'm not here because I flunked out of chemistry at my old school."

His easy laugh made Stevie cringe. *What am I, invisible?* she thought irritably. *Scott is chatting away with Sue as if they were alone at this table.*

"Callie's really terrific," Scott went on, leaning a little closer to Sue as if he were about to divulge some intriguing secret. "Back home, she won all kinds of awards for her horseback riding. Do you ride, Sue?"

"No," Sue said. She glanced over at Stevie. "Stevie does, though. Don't you, Stevie?"

Stevie stiffened as Scott glanced at her. The only thing worse than being ignored by him was facing his cold, unwavering gaze. "Uh-huh," she managed to say.

Scott nodded. "Right." Then he returned his attention to Sue. "But anyway, I've just been blabbing on and on about myself. Why don't you tell me a little bit about yourself?" He gave another of his charming, totally unself-conscious laughs. "After all, if we're going to be lab partners, we ought to get to know each other."

Stevie sighed and slumped on her stool. This was shaping up to be a very painful semester.

Carole picked at a peeling spot of paint on the fence of the schooling ring as she watched Ben ride Firefly in a tight circle. The young dapple gray mare shook her head impatiently as Ben turned her in the opposite direction and walked her toward the far end of the ring.

As usual, Carole found herself admiring Ben's confident, well-balanced seat and the way he handled the horse. It sometimes seemed to her as if the young stable hand spoke to horses in their own language. How else could she explain the way they responded to him? *Well, most of them, anyway,* Carole thought as Firefly arched her neck, shook her head again, and did her best to whirl away from the path Ben wanted her to follow. Firefly was new to Pine Hollow, and her training was still in its early stages. Spirited and high-strung, she required a lot of patience from her trainers.

Unfortunately, Carole wasn't feeling especially patient at that moment. She had been planning to school Samson over a jump course that she had worked out in her head during her last three classes.

It hadn't been until she had arrived at Pine Hollow and found Ben waiting for her in the tack room that she remembered: They had made plans for a long training session with Firefly. Samson would have to wait.

Carole sighed and flicked one more speck of paint off the rail in front of her as Ben brought Firefly to a halt. They were facing away from Carole, but she could tell by the horse's flicking ears that Ben was talking softly to her. After a moment, he asked her to walk again. This time Firefly responded immediately. But when he tried to bring her around the end of the ring at a trot, she broke into a choppy canter and then danced off to the side, snorting loudly.

Ben spoke to her firmly, then managed to steer her toward the spot where Carole was watching. "She's really feeling her oats today," Ben said, sounding a little breathless.

"I can tell." Carole watched the mare. Carole was having trouble concentrating on Firefly, but she knew she had a responsibility to Max. He had asked her to help train this horse, too, and Carole took that responsibility seriously. She ran her eyes over the frisky young mare, trying to figure out what to do. "It looks like you're having trouble keeping her attention. Do you think she's not getting enough exercise?"

Ben shrugged. "I think she's just flighty and easily distracted," he said. "I wonder if working her alongside another horse would help steady her. Why don't you go tack up Starlight and we'll give it a try?"

"I've got an even better idea!" Carole said quickly. "I was planning to put Samson over some low jumps like these later anyway. Why don't I go get him now?"

Ben looked dubious. "Samson?"

"Sure." Carole smiled. "It'll be fun."

"Samson isn't all that much older than Firefly," Ben pointed out, frowning slightly.

"Don't worry." Carole didn't let him finish. She was already turning away. "I'll be out in a jiff."

Ben shrugged. "Whatever."

Carole noticed that he still didn't look convinced. *But he'll see,* she told herself as she rushed inside. *He just doesn't know Samson the way I do. This will work out great.*

"Whoa! Steady, big guy." Carole's voice and hands were firm as she brought Samson to a halt. The big black horse let out a snort and rolled his eyes in the direction of Firefly, who was prancing nervously nearby, tossing her head wildly as Ben fought for control.

Samson flicked his ears back toward Carole, and

she let out a quick sigh of relief. He was still listening to her, and that was good. All he needed was a little time to work out his energy, and then they could begin this training session in earnest.

"Are you okay?" Ben called to her.

Glancing over, Carole saw that he had Firefly standing more or less calmly by the fence. "Fine," she called back. "Samson is just enthusiastic, that's all. He hasn't spent much time with other horses since he got here." She made a mental note to fix that, chastising herself for not thinking of it sooner. Samson needed to be able to work calmly in the presence of other horses, and he was proving that he was out of practice with that.

Carole had to admit—to herself, if not to Ben— that this training session wasn't going smoothly so far. Ever since Samson had entered the ring, he had been more interested in showing off for the gray mare than doing what Carole wanted him to do. The two young horses were both just excitable enough to get each other completely riled up.

Still, Carole was sure that after the two of them had spent a few minutes working out their high spirits, they would be able to work together just fine. She just hoped Ben would have enough patience to wait it out.

"It's okay, Samson," she said soothingly as her horse took a few quick steps sideways. "I know you want to play. But we've got to get to work soon." She cast a worried glance across the ring.

Ben was speaking softly to Firefly. The mare listened at first, her ears tilted back toward her rider. But then Samson let out a loud snort, and Firefly danced around to face him, stamping her slender forelegs and nickering.

Samson tossed his head, snorted again, and whirled around before Carole could stop him. He was halfway across the ring, trotting away from Firefly, before she managed to command his attention once more. "Okay, big fella," she told him. "That's enough. Do you want that mare to think you don't have any manners?"

Ben rode toward her. "Maybe this isn't such a good idea. . . ."

"It's okay," Carole answered immediately, turning Samson to face Firefly. For once, both horses stood more or less calmly as their riders talked. "See? They're settling down." She grinned. "They were just excited about working together."

Ben shrugged. "If you say so."

"I do say so," Carole replied tartly, feeling almost as spirited as Samson. "Come on, let's try them over the course now. I'll go first."

Ben nodded, and Carole clucked to Samson, wheeling him around to make a circuit of the ring. All she had to do was get him moving smoothly and concentrating on his work. Then she could take him to the first fence, and . . .

Samson had other ideas. He trotted smoothly enough the first time around the ring. But when Carole brought him around past Firefly, he broke stride and darted toward her, stretching his head out playfully. The mare responded by whirling away and half rearing, then dancing sideways and shaking her head so hard that Ben had trouble holding on to the reins.

"Whoa!" Carole cried, dismayed. "Samson, calm down!"

After a few minutes Carole and Ben managed to get both horses standing quietly again, though Samson kept turning to stare at Firefly, and the gray mare continued to stamp one foot occasionally.

"This isn't working," Ben said bluntly, his face sweaty from exertion. "They're getting more unmanageable by the minute."

Ben was right. He had been patient—they both had—but it was clear that Samson and Firefly weren't ready to work together. She sighed, feeling unreasonably disappointed. "What do you think we should do?" she asked heavily. "Should I go put Samson away and tack up Starlight?"

Ben responded by dismounting. "I don't think so," he said once he was on the ground with Firefly firmly in hand. "This girl needs to get away from here for a while and calm down."

"Oh." Carole bit her lip as she thought about all the work she had planned to do with Samson that day. Now it would have to wait even longer while she helped soothe the excitable mare. "All right. I'll help you walk her. It might take two of us."

Ben shrugged. "It's okay. I'll handle it," he said. "You might as well stay here and keep working with Samson now that he's warmed up."

Carole's heart soared. But she tried not to look as happy as she felt. She didn't want Ben to think she was shirking her duties to Firefly. "Are you sure? I can help if you need it. Really."

"I'll be fine." Ben turned and led the mare away, closing the subject.

Carole shrugged and smiled as she watched them go. "Thanks," she called. There was no response from Ben, but she wasn't really expecting one. Besides, she knew he was probably right. Firefly was so flighty that it would be better for all of them simply to put her away for the day and let her settle down. Ben would probably untack her and then walk her around the empty back paddock to cool and calm her. That would be the best thing for her, but it really wasn't a two-person job. Ben could handle it, and Carole was free to turn her full attention to Samson.

"Ready, fella?" she murmured to the horse, who calmed down quite a bit once Firefly disappeared inside. "Let's get to work."

Forty minutes later, Carole reluctantly pulled Samson to a halt. "That was great," she told him with a pat. "I think your mama must have been part kangaroo."

She was feeling a little giddy, but then again, why shouldn't she? The training session had been terrific. Samson had done everything she had asked and more, making her wonder if there was anything this horse couldn't do. She would have liked to go on riding all afternoon—riding out of the ring, cross-country, jumping everything in their path— but she knew it was time to stop. Samson didn't seem tired yet, but she wasn't about to take any chances with Max's new champ.

She slid off the horse's back and led him out of the ring. He needed to be walked after the strenuous workout, but the late-afternoon sun was so hot that Carole decided it would be more comfortable to walk him in the shade of the indoor ring. She headed inside.

As she approached the door to the indoor ring, she saw that it was propped open, and it sounded as if the ring was occupied. Carole frowned, disappointed, and glanced at her watch. There were no beginning or intermediate lessons scheduled this late in the day.

Keeping a firm grip on Samson's lead, she approached the door and peered inside. What she saw didn't register at first, and she wrinkled her nose, confused.

Red O'Malley was mounted on Topside, who was cantering across the center of the ring, heading for a low jump just ahead. To one side, Ben sat aboard Firefly. The gray mare was standing calmly and her ears were pricked forward as she watched Topside move past. Carole backed away from the door, her forehead creased as she wondered what was going on.

In a flash, she understood. Ben had gone ahead with his plan without her, without even telling her. He had lied. He had let her think he was taking Firefly in when actually he had enlisted Red to help him instead of Carole.

Why? she asked herself, staring blankly ahead as Firefly came forward and started cantering smoothly next to Topside as he passed her again. The well-trained older horse didn't so much as acknowledge the mare's presence, and after flicking her ears toward him a few times, Firefly ignored Topside just as completely.

Carole felt her face turning red. Ben had lied to her. He had tricked her, rejected the help she had offered, and then sought the same help from someone else. Feeling angry and betrayed, she whirled around and hurried away, with Samson in tow, before either of the other riders could see her standing there.

THIRTEEN

"I'm coming, I'm coming," Stevie chanted under her breath as she hurried down the sidewalk on Wednesday afternoon, dodging baby strollers and recently released students from the nearby elementary school. She glanced at her watch and gulped. Phil had been on her case a lot lately about being late, and even though she had a perfectly good excuse—her after-school student council meeting had run late because of a heated debate over the junior-class fund-raiser—she hated to prove him right.

She sped up as she approached the corner of Magnolia and Broad in downtown Willow Creek. Taking the corner at a fast jog, she headed for a tiny side street at the far end of the town's original shopping district. Stevie knew the occupants of each turn-of-the-century brick storefront without bothering to look—HiValu Shoes, the fire station, an accountant's office, Old Dixie Hardware Emporium, Stevie's dentist's office. Things didn't change much in downtown Willow Creek. There had been what passed for an uproar when the flower shop on State Street had closed and been replaced by a McDonald's—in other words, several crusty old ladies had written politely scathing protest letters to the local newspaper, and the mayor, who doubled as the town's most popular barber, had said a few disapproving words at a town meeting about the evils of the modern world.

Stevie didn't waste much time thinking about any of that as she raced along the wide sidewalk beneath the shade of red maples that were just beginning to show hints of their bright autumn foliage, though she did spare a moment of thanks that her favorite bakery, Deanna's, hadn't changed its jelly doughnut recipe in the last fifty-odd years. She could already taste the sweet, sugary treat, with its surprisingly tart interior . . . She just hoped Phil hadn't decided to teach her a lesson by buying and eating every doughnut in the place while he was waiting for her.

That thought made her put on one final burst of speed as she reached the corner. But once she'd taken the turn she skidded to a stop, brought up short by the scene in front of Deanna's, halfway down the block. Phil was leaning against the sun-warmed brick wall just outside the bakery door. Straddling a bicycle on the cracked sidewalk in front of the bakery, leaning back comfortably on the seat as he talked to Phil, was Scott Forester. As Stevie watched, Scott threw his head back and laughed loudly at something Phil had just said.

Stevie felt her whole body tighten up. Seeing Scott there was a surprise, and not a pleasant one. She'd had her fill of him for the past couple of days in chemistry class, where he continued to ignore her as much as possible. What was he doing there now, talking to her boyfriend?

Don't get all worked up about nothing, Stevie told herself as she walked slowly toward the two boys. *Tons of kids come to Deanna's after school.*

Still, she couldn't help an uneasy flash of déjà vu as she watched the two boys standing there, talking and laughing with each other. It was just like the other time, at the stable . . . and it gave her the same uncomfortable mishmash of feelings.

She took a few tentative steps forward. Soon she was close enough to hear what Phil and Scott were saying. The street was crowded enough that they still hadn't noticed her approaching.

". . . and so I was thinking," Scott was saying. "I've hardly used the basketball hoop Dad and I put up when we moved in. Maybe we can get a few guys together for a friendly game this weekend." Stevie noticed that Scott's deep, jovial voice had a way of carrying, even though he didn't seem to be speaking loudly. She wondered if that was some kind of politician's trick he'd picked up from his father.

Phil's voice wasn't quite as audible, but Stevie was so attuned to it that she didn't have any trouble making out what he said in reply.

"Sounds cool," he said eagerly. "Count me in."

Stevie's breath caught in her throat. The Redskins game had been one thing—she couldn't blame Phil for wanting to see his favorite team in action, no matter who he was going with. But this? This was more like the kind of casual plans a couple of *friends* might make.

Just then Phil turned his head and spotted her. Stevie couldn't help noticing, even now, that Phil's eyes still lit up every time he saw her, just as she suspected her own did when she saw him. But this time, when he made a move to greet her with his usual quick kiss, she turned her head to avoid it. For some reason she didn't feel like kissing him in front of Scott. Not right then, after what she had just heard. It was too weird.

Phil looked surprised, but he didn't comment on her dodge. Instead he slung one arm around her shoulder and glanced at Scott. "Stevie and I are going to stuff ourselves with as many doughnuts as we can hold," he told him. "Want to join us?"

"No thanks," Scott said, responding just a little too quickly. "Mom's having some kind of club meeting tonight, and if I don't get home with these croissants soon, she'll have my hide." He held up a white paper bag and shook it slightly. "See you later."

"Bye." Phil waved and smiled as Scott pedaled away. Then he turned his gaze to Stevie. "Ready to pig out?" A flicker of surprise passed over his face as he met Stevie's glare. "What's the matter?"

"Nothing," she replied, looking away. She gulped in a few deep breaths. She wasn't about to let Scott Forester be the cause of a fight. *He's not worth it,* she told herself firmly. *Let it go.* "Come on. I'm starving."

Phil seemed about to press the point, but then he shrugged and allowed Stevie to lead the way into the dim, sweet-smelling bakery. The long narrow store was largely taken up by a huge display case crowded with all sorts of delicious-looking cookies, cakes, and pies. Behind the counter, several flour-dusted workers hurried to fill the customers' orders, while Deanna herself—granddaughter of the place's original namesake—oversaw everything from her stool behind the cash register.

Stevie and Phil placed their order and received a bag stuffed with fresh-from-the-fryer doughnuts. As they waited for their change, Stevie grabbed a jelly doughnut from the top of the bag and took a big bite. As soon as she tasted it, she felt a little better.

What was the big deal, really? Stevie should be glad that Scott wanted to hang out with Phil. Maybe it meant he would soon lighten up on Stevie, too— and maybe she wouldn't have to dread sixth period quite so much every day. *Well, maybe I wouldn't go that far,* she added to herself with a private laugh.

She gave Phil a big smile to prove nothing was wrong. "Mmm," she said, taking another bite of her doughnut. "This hits the spot."

Phil chuckled and wiped a streak of powdered sugar off her chin. "Did anyone ever tell you that you look cute with food all over your face?"

At that moment the little bell over the front door tinkled, and when Stevie glanced over she spotted a familiar pretty face entering the store. "Julianna," she called out in surprise. A.J.'s ex-girlfriend—it was still hard for Stevie to think of her that way, even though two weeks had passed since the breakup— seemed somehow out of place there in Willow Creek, especially on a school day and miles from Pine Hollow.

Phil had been busy taking his change from De-anna. But as he stepped away from the register, he looked just as surprised as Stevie felt. "What a coincidence!" he exclaimed, hurrying toward Julianna with Stevie on his heels. "What are you doing here?"

Julianna gave them both a smile that looked a bit

forced. "It's no coincidence," she admitted, glancing at Phil. "Actually, I stopped by your house looking for you, and your sister told me you might be here."

Stevie couldn't get over the change in Julianna's appearance since the last time she'd seen her. She wouldn't have believed that anything could dampen Julianna's sunny spirits, but now she looked downright depressed. Even her glorious wavy red hair seemed less bright and bouncy than usual.

"Well, you found me." Phil smiled encouragingly at Julianna. "What's up?"

Julianna glanced around at the other customers. "Can we talk somewhere more private?" she asked hesitantly.

"Sure." Stevie took her arm and steered her toward the door. Once outside, she led the way across the street to a small, half-empty parking lot.

The three of them perched on the low wall enclosing the lot, with Julianna in the middle. Stevie offered the other girl a doughnut, and Julianna accepted, nibbling daintily at the edge and somehow managing to avoid getting even a speck of powdered sugar on her face. Stevie couldn't help wrinkling her nose slightly when she noticed that. Julianna was the type of girl who never seemed to get dirty or sweaty or rumpled—and that was a type Stevie just couldn't understand. Where was the fun in always being neat and pretty? Still, she felt sorry for Julianna as she noticed her red-rimmed eyes. It seemed that even neat, pretty girls with bouncy, perfect hair could get hurt and upset sometimes.

"How are you doing?" she asked Julianna carefully, not sure what to say. "I haven't seen you since that day at the creek."

Julianna blinked hard a few times. "I know," she said softly. "That seems like years ago now." She glanced from Stevie to Phil and back again. "I'm sorry to barge in on you guys like this. You probably have plans and everything. But I—I really need someone to talk to, and I just didn't know who else—"

Phil put a hand on her arm. "It's okay," he said soothingly. "We understand. This has been tough on all of us."

Stevie felt a swelling of pride as she watched her boyfriend comfort Julianna. Phil could be so sensitive and understanding—it was just one of the many things she loved about him.

Julianna seemed to appreciate it, too. She managed another faint smile. "Thanks." She stared down at the half-eaten doughnut in her hand. "It's just so weird, you know? I mean, I'm crazy about A.J., and I thought he felt the same way about me. And then this . . ."

Stevie shifted her weight on the wall, torn between curiosity and politeness. Curiosity won. "Didn't you see this coming at all?" she blurted out. "I mean, I know it's none of my business. But was anything—you know—wrong? Before, I mean."

Phil shot Stevie a warning look over Julianna's bowed head, but if Julianna was taken aback she didn't show it. "Nothing was wrong," she replied. "Nothing that I knew about, anyway. I mean, we never had a lot of deep conversations or anything. But I thought we were tight enough that he would let me know if he was unhappy." She started blinking again. "And I never would have guessed he would break things off like this—without any explanation, any warning. I tried to be patient, you know, give him a week or two to cool off so that we could maybe discuss it or whatever, but he still won't talk to me or even look at me when I pass him in the halls."

"If it's any comfort, none of us would have guessed this was coming, either," Phil told her. "A.J. seemed really happy with you. And he's not acting like himself with any of his friends. So this might not really even be about you or your relationship."

Stevie glanced at Phil in surprise. She hadn't thought about it that way before, and she wasn't sure Phil should be getting Julianna's hopes up like that, making her think the breakup had been a result rather than a cause of A.J.'s behavior. Then again, Phil knew A.J. better than anyone. Maybe there was more to this bad mood of his than Stevie had realized.

She glanced at Julianna. She still wasn't sure exactly why she was here, but it was clear she was hurting, and that made Stevie wonder even more. Stevie had known A.J. for years, and she had always thought of him as one of the kindest and most considerate guys she had ever met. Once when his horse, Crystal, had come down with a bad case of colic, A.J. had stayed up with her for two nights running, soothing her and singing to her to keep her mind off her discomfort. That was the kind of person he was—the kind of person she could easily imagine someone falling in love with, but not the kind of person she could imagine breaking Julianna's heart.

"Listen, Julianna," Stevie said, feeling a sudden rush of sympathy for the girl. "Phil and I were just going to head over to my house and hang out— nothing exciting. But you're welcome to come with us. How about it?"

"That's okay." Julianna stood and smiled at them. "It's been a big help just talking to you guys like this." She glanced at her watch. "I'd better get home."

"Take care." Phil watched her as she walked off

toward the busy main street. When she rounded the corner and disappeared from sight, he turned to Stevie with a worried sigh. "Wow. I wouldn't have guessed she'd take it this hard."

"I know," Stevie agreed. "I guess it's hard when you don't even know what went wrong." She scooted closer to Phil on the wall and slipped her hand into his, shuddering at the thought of how lonely it would be if the person you thought loved you suddenly stopped talking to you—and you didn't even know why.

Phil nodded and squeezed her hand. But when Stevie glanced at him, his expression was grim as he stared off in the direction Julianna had gone. "It's just not like him," he muttered, his voice low and confused. "It's not like him at all."

Stevie squeezed back, feeling sympathetic but helpless at the same time. It was obvious that Phil was hurting almost as much as Julianna was, and Stevie didn't think she could do anything to help them. Nobody could. *Except A.J. himself, of course,* she added to herself. *And that doesn't look likely right now.*

She sighed. Up until then, she had assumed that A.J. was going through a phase, that there had been more to the breakup story than they knew, that there had been some kind of problem with Julianna that none of them had seen. But after seeing Julianna, she was having trouble believing that any-more.

The next Monday, Stevie hurried out of chemis-try class as fast as her legs would take her, her fists clenched beneath the stack of books she was carry-ing. A week had passed since they had begun work-ing with their lab groups, but to Stevie it felt more like a year. Or maybe a decade.

There's only one thing worse than putting up with Scott's attitude every afternoon in lab, Stevie thought glumly as she eased her way into the throng of stu-dents rushing to get to their seventh-period classes. *And that's watching him whoop it up with Phil every time they see each other at Pine Hollow.*

She sighed with frustration as she thought about it. As difficult as it still was for her to believe, let alone accept, Scott and Phil actually seemed to be becoming friends. That was bad enough. Worse was that, aside from their encounter at the bakery the week before, Pine Hollow seemed to be their com-mon meeting ground. They had run into each other one day at the stable when Scott had arrived to pick up Callie at the same time Phil had dropped by to see Stevie, and they had ended up involved in a lively half-hour political discussion. Then Scott had asked Phil to take a look at his computer, which was giving him some trouble, and the two of them had driven off to the Foresters' with hardly a backward glance for Stevie. And finally, just the day before, Stevie had spotted Scott's car pulling into the drive to pick up Phil for a game of tennis at Willow Creek Country Club, which Scott's family had just joined.

It was almost too much for Stevie to take. Pine Hollow had always been a sort of sanctuary to her—a place where she could escape the noisy pressures of her large family, worries about school, or just about anything else. A place where she could relax, have fun, and just be herself. Even though her brother Alex had started spending more time there, it had still remained a safe haven, a special spot of her own, the one place where she always felt she belonged.

Now that was changing. And it was all Scott's fault.

Why couldn't her boyfriend see how much this was bothering her? She knew that he was very upset about A.J., and she could understand that perfectly well, but was that an excuse for ignoring her feelings? It wasn't as though she was very good at hiding them. And Scott was no better, of course—whenever he saw her, whether at the stable or in class, he merely nodded and then avoided any further eye contact or direct address. Despite Stevie's former hopes, Scott's friendship with Phil didn't seem to be thawing Scott's feelings toward her one iota.

Stevie walked slowly down the hall, lost in thought, forcing the rushing students to find a way around her. The awkward situation at Pine Hollow was bad enough. Then there was her chemistry grade to worry about.

She sighed and shifted her books to her other arm. Thanks to their total lack of meaningful communication, she and Scott had managed to mess up one lab already. On the next one, only Sue's quick intervention had headed off complete disaster. It was obvious that poor Sue had no idea what was going on between her two lab partners, but it was equally obvious that she was too shy to confront them about it.

Stevie had no idea what to do. She didn't want to flunk chemistry any more than she wanted to have to slink around Pine Hollow like some kind of intruder. But until Scott decided to change his attitude, what choice did she have? It was all very well to make vows about not letting other people control your life. Sometimes, though, it was hard to see how to keep those vows.

Reaching her locker, Stevie twirled the combination lock automatically, her mind still focused on her problems. *What are my options here?* she asked herself as she yanked the locker door open and added her chemistry books to the jumble inside. *There's got to be something I can do. Things can't go on this way.*

She paused, staring into the locker and thinking hard. One thing she knew for sure—she wasn't about to beg Scott to forgive her for what had happened to Callie. They had been through that already.

I could ask Ms. Rourke to switch me to another lab group, Stevie thought, not for the first time that week. That seemed like one of the more practical and satisfying options she had come up with. *Of course, walking up to Scott and punching him in the nose would be pretty satisfying, too. And why not? It couldn't make things between us much worse.*

Suddenly remembering where she was, Stevie started digging through the contents of her locker, searching for her American history notebook. If she didn't hurry, she would be late for seventh period.

And that would be Scott's fault, too, she thought irritably. It was unbelievable how much energy she wasted these days thinking and worrying about Scott. Scott and Phil. Scott and chemistry. Scott and *everything*. It didn't seem fair. Weren't these supposed to be the best days of her life?

She finally located her notebook and yanked it out. "They sure don't feel that great," she muttered angrily, slamming her locker shut and whirling around.

"Whoa!" a familiar voice behind her said. "Watch it, Stevie."

Stevie immediately saw that she had almost barreled into Callie, who was standing behind her. "Oh. Sorry. I didn't see you there."

"Obviously." Callie peered into her face. "Are you okay? You don't look so good."

"I don't *feel* so good," Stevie countered, brushing back her hair with one hand and trying to maintain control of her emotions. Sometimes a sympathetic face was harder to take than an unfriendly one, and this was one of those times.

Callie hesitated. "Does this by any chance have something to do with my brother?" she asked quietly. "I mean, I know you just got out of chemistry . . ."

Stevie turned and started walking down the hall toward her next class. Callie kept pace, swinging her metal crutches expertly. "Since you ask," Stevie said, "your brother is driving me nuts."

Callie nodded understandingly. "I don't blame you for being upset about that. I have to admit, I don't get it myself. Scott isn't usually weird like this. So I don't know what to tell you." She sighed, sounding so frustrated that Stevie glanced at her in surprise.

"Are you okay?" Stevie asked, for the first time noting the worried crease in Callie's forehead. "Now that I think about it, you aren't looking so hot right now yourself."

Callie shrugged. "It's nothing," she replied. "Much." For a moment that seemed to be all she had to say. Then she went on, speaking so quietly that Stevie had trouble hearing her over the noise of the students in the hallway. "I had a doctor's appointment today during lunch. I asked Dr. Amandsen when he thought I could ditch these." She gestured to her crutches.

"What did he say?"

Callie sighed and lowered her eyes. "He said it was too soon to be talking about that yet." Her disappointment was audible.

Stevie understood and searched her mind for a way to help. But there was no time. She knew the seventh-period bell would be ringing any second. "Listen," she said. "We've both got to get to class. But why don't we meet up afterward and head over to TD's? It seems like we could both stand to drown our problems in ice cream."

Callie glanced over at her and cracked a smile. "You know, I think you may be right about that," she said. "It's a date."

". . . and then this other time, I decided to go all out," Stevie said, waving her spoon for emphasis. "I told the waitress to mix together all the toppings she had in a blender and dump them on top of the ice cream." She leaned back in the booth and grinned. "Believe me, if looks could kill, I wouldn't be here talking to you right now."

Callie laughed. It was amazing how much her mood had changed since the doctor's appointment earlier that day. She and Stevie had met after school as planned and come straight to the little ice cream parlor. The place wasn't crowded, so the two of them had snagged the best booth and ordered sundaes. Callie had wrinkled her nose at Stevie's choice of sundae—butterscotch on banana ice cream—and ever since, Stevie had been entertaining her with tales of the much more outrageous ice cream combinations she had loved to order when she was younger. Apparently it had been quite a hobby of hers to go out of her way to disgust the waitress who had worked there back then, which, to Callie, sounded just exactly like something Stevie might do.

It's amazing how much of a difference it can make to just sit around and laugh instead of worrying about things, Callie told herself. Just a few hours earlier, Dr. Amandsen had told her it wasn't realistic to think about losing her crutches any time before

Thanksgiving, no matter how hard she worked. Callie had been ready to rush home, bury her head in her pillow, and give up. That wasn't like her, she knew. Normally a challenge like that would have made her buckle down and work twice as hard to prove the doctor wrong. Hadn't she done exactly that by making such fast progress in her therapeutic riding? *But this time it's different,* she thought dejectedly. *This time hard work may not be enough. . . .*

She let the thought drop. She would just have to figure out how to deal with this situation somehow.

Stevie was still talking. ". . . and so the waitress refused to do it, and I was ready to make her call out the manager." She grinned and shrugged. "But Lisa and Carole talked me out of it. They even offered to pay if I'd order a normal sundae and leave the waitress alone."

Callie chuckled. "I probably would have made the same offer," she admitted. "Still, it sounds like you three have always had a lot of fun together."

"Yes, we have," Stevie said. "The three of us used to spend absolutely all our time together. We must have had sleepovers at each other's houses at least once a week, and we even spent a lot of our vacations together." She slurped a bit of melted ice cream off her spoon. "So whenever Alex starts complaining about how Lisa spends more time with me than with him—which is so not true, by the way, since he totally hogs her attention—I just remind him it could be a lot worse."

Stevie chattered on about her past adventures with her friends. Callie continued to listen, sipping her water, eating her ice cream, and laughing in all the right places. But she was starting to feel a little uncomfortable, as she often did when Stevie or Carole or Lisa started talking about all the fun times they'd had together in the past. It was hard not to feel like an outsider sometimes when they started reminiscing, no matter how careful they were to include her in the conversation.

True, those feelings had decreased over the months as she had gotten more comfortable with Stevie and Carole. But Callie felt them welling up now, stronger than they'd been in a long time.

I bet I know exactly why that is, Callie told herself ruefully, glancing down at the crutches leaning against her seat. But she veered away from that thought, unwilling to explore it further until she had to. Instead, she wished for the millionth time in her life that her father could be happy with an ordinary job like other fathers had. It would be so nice not to have to watch everything she said and did because her family was in the public eye, to be able to have close, caring, long-term friendships like the ones Stevie and Carole and Lisa had with each other without worrying so much about people's motives . . .

She bit back a sigh and did her best not to let her emotions show as she returned her attention to Stevie, who was in the middle of talking about some horse show or other that she and her friends had helped organize.

It must be so wonderful to be normal, Callie thought wistfully.

"I'm starting to feel paranoid," Lisa told Alex as they strolled toward the shopping center. It was another hot September afternoon, and Lisa had just driven them over from the stable. "No matter how many times I ask Max what's going on with Prancer, he just keeps telling me she's 'under observation.' What on earth does that mean?"

Alex reached for her hand and squeezed it. "You asked me that already. Six times, I think. And I still don't know."

"Sorry." Lisa shot him an apologetic smile. His tone was mild, but she knew he was probably genuinely sick of talking about this. Somehow, though, she just couldn't seem to drop it. "I wish I knew what was going on," she murmured, thinking back over the week. She had only had time to get over to Pine Hollow twice, but both times she had found that Prancer was off-limits and nobody would tell her why. It was really starting to scare her. What could be so terrible that Max wouldn't even talk about it?

Alex swung his arm, moving their joined hands back and forth between them as they walked. "I thought you talked to Carole about this."

"I did." Lisa ran her free hand through her hair, lifting it off the nape of her neck to cool herself. "I talked to her a couple of days ago. She still claims everything's fine."

Alex raised one eyebrow questioningly. " 'Claims'? " he repeated. "That makes it sound like you didn't believe her."

"I did believe her at first." Lisa sighed. "But after today . . ."

Alex gave a slow, puzzled shrug. They had reached the sidewalk that ran the length of the storefronts, and he turned to face her. "I'm trying to be supportive here, Lisa," he said. "But to be honest, I'm still not even sure what you're worried about."

"I'm not sure, either." Lisa stared at the ground. "I mean, Prancer doesn't look sick." She sighed and met Alex's sympathetic eyes. "I know I'm probably just being silly." Forcing a slight laugh, she added, "For all I know, Max could be doing this on purpose to get me to ride different horses, like you said.

He does get kind of hyper about his riders getting lots of experience."

Alex reached out to brush a strand of hair off her cheek and smiled at her. "You probably shouldn't worry about this too much. If there was anything important going on, Carole would have told you. She wouldn't lie to you."

Three weeks ago Lisa would have automatically agreed with him about that. But today, she couldn't keep a tiny sliver of doubt from wiggling its way into her mind. Best friends didn't lie to each other. They didn't keep secrets. Did they?

Lisa sighed again as she and Alex continued toward TD's. She tried to tell herself, as she had been doing for the past couple of weeks, that she was just getting worked up about nothing. But that was getting harder and harder for her to believe. It was true that Max could sometimes get so caught up in stable business, he forgot that people couldn't read his mind. Come to think of it, the same could be said about Carole. But this time, Lisa couldn't quite convince herself that that was all that was going on.

And she didn't like that thought at all, mostly because the possibilities were too terrifying. After all, Prancer wasn't anywhere near old enough to be retiring. And Max surely wasn't selling her—actually, that was least likely of all, since Judy Barker was part owner of the horse. And the last time Lisa had seen Judy, at the dry cleaner's a couple of days after returning from California, Judy had asked after Prancer and commented on how well suited the mare and Pine Hollow were to each other. That didn't seem like the comment of a woman who was thinking about selling her horse.

Unless she's selling her half of Prancer to Max, Lisa thought suddenly, her heart lifting. That idea hadn't occurred to her before. But it made a lot of sense. Maybe Max was buying out Judy's ownership of the mare. The lovely Thoroughbred had been a wonderful riding horse over the years since she had come to Pine Hollow—why shouldn't Max decide that he wanted to own her outright? And why shouldn't Judy agree to that? She wasn't really getting much out of her half of the deal, and she knew Max would take good care of Prancer. . . .

Lisa smiled as she and Alex walked along, feeling relieved. She was sure she had figured out the truth. It was so obvious that she couldn't believe she hadn't seen it before. It explained why Max was being so secretive. It had nothing to do with Prancer's health after all, as Lisa had feared. *At least I hope not,* a suspicious little voice inside her said. But she squashed that voice and held on to her new optimism.

"After you," Alex announced, pulling open the door of TD's and holding it for Lisa.

"Thanks." Lisa stepped into the ice cream parlor, still caught up in her thoughts.

But Alex was scanning the small room. "Hey, check it out," he said. "There's my dorky sister, gulping down ice cream as if her life depended on it."

"Stevie's here?" Lisa smiled. But when she followed Alex's gaze to the corner booth on the back wall, her heart sank. Stevie wasn't alone, and she wasn't with Carole or Phil. She was with Callie. The two of them were leaning forward over half-empty ice cream dishes, deep in conversation.

Lisa's first instinct was to leave before they spotted her. But Alex had already grabbed her arm and was dragging her forward.

"Yo!" he called. "How's it going, guys? Got room for two more?"

Stevie looked up, smiled, and waved. "I don't know," she joked. "We definitely have room for Lisa. But as for you . . ."

Alex rolled his eyes and shoved Stevie aside. Plopping onto the vinyl seat next to her, he leaned over and gave her a big, sloppy kiss on the cheek. "Thanks, sister dear," he said. "I love you, too."

Stevie wiped her face, pretending to be disgusted, but she was having trouble keeping a straight face.

Meanwhile, Callie looked up at Lisa and smiled. "Have a seat," she invited, moving her crutches and sliding over to make room beside her.

Lisa smiled back and sat down. "Thanks." She felt a little uncomfortable, though she was trying not to let it show. She hadn't been prepared to run into Callie right then. And she didn't like feeling unprepared.

After flagging down a waiter, Alex settled back in his seat. "So what were you two gabbing about when we got here?" he asked Stevie and Callie.

"How ugly you are," Stevie replied promptly.

Callie smiled. "She's kidding, Alex," she said. "Actually, we were just talking about Phil's friend A.J."

"That's right," Stevie admitted, sounding much more serious. "Phil has been so upset he never seems to talk about anything else anymore. Callie was just helping me figure out how to handle that and make him feel better."

Callie shrugged. "I don't know how much help I've really been," she said modestly. "I just told Stevie she had to let Phil work through this. He's complaining so much to her because he can't talk it out with A.J. So all Stevie can really do to help him is be supportive and let him talk whenever he needs to."

Lisa was liking this conversation less and less. It

had nothing to do with A.J. and his problems, whatever they might be, and everything to do with Callie. It wasn't that Callie's advice to Stevie wasn't good. On the contrary, it sounded very much like what Lisa might have said herself—if she'd been asked.

And that was what was really bothering her. Once upon a time she would have been asked— Stevie had always discussed these sorts of problems with her and Carole. *Only* her and Carole. Now she was sharing her life with Callie, too. And Callie seemed all too comfortable in the role of pragmatic, responsible friend—the same role Lisa had always filled—to the often impulsive and irresponsible Stevie. Lisa didn't like the implications of that. She didn't like them at all.

She had to head off those kinds of thoughts before she gave herself away. The last thing she wanted to do was cause a scene. The waiter arrived at that moment with their orders, so Lisa had a few moments to collect herself.

When the waiter had left, she turned to her seat-mate. "So, Callie," she said brightly, remembering their discussion at the barbecue a couple of weeks earlier. "Have you heard any more about that friend of yours? You know, the one you said might be coming to visit?"

"You mean Sheila?" Stevie asked, reaching over to

snitch the cherry from the top of Alex's sundae. She was kind of relieved that Lisa had changed the subject. She was tired of talking about Phil and A.J.

"I guess so," said Lisa. Callie licked her spoon and set it carefully back in the empty ice cream dish. "Yes, it looks like she's coming in a week or so. I can't wait."

"That's nice. Were you two friends for a long time?" Lisa asked politely.

Callie nodded. "I've known her forever."

"That's great." Lisa took another bite of ice cream. "You must be very excited."

"I am," Callie agreed. "Definitely."

Stevie finishing chewing her stolen cherry and glanced around the table. She couldn't put her finger on it, but there was something a little off about this conversation.

Alex was busy shoveling his sundae into his mouth and seemed a lot more interested in the chocolate ice cream and marshmallow sauce than in anything the girls were saying. Stevie turned her attention to Lisa and Callie.

Neither of her friends looked comfortable. Callie was squeezed so far over in the booth that her shoulder was pressed against the wall, and Lisa, seeming just as eager to keep plenty of space between them, was perched at the very edge of the seat. They were talking to each other politely enough, but they never quite seemed to meet each other's eyes.

Stevie frowned. She realized that Lisa and Callie didn't know each other all that well, since they went to different schools. Still, they had hit it off well enough at the beginning of the summer before Lisa had left for California. And they were both such good friends with her and Carole that it only made sense they'd like each other. . . .

"What's Sheila like?" Lisa asked.

Callie shrugged and toyed with her napkin. "Oh, you know. She's smart, she's nice—you'll probably meet her while she's here. She rides, and she's already made me promise to show her around Pine Hollow."

Stevie's eyes narrowed as she listened. While she recognized that not everyone was as exuberant as she was, she still thought Callie didn't sound as if she was looking forward to Sheila's visit very much. In fact, she seemed rather reluctant to talk about it.

At that moment Alex looked up from his ice cream. "Gross," he announced, poking around with his spoon. "I told them to hold the walnuts."

"I'll take them," Stevie offered. She held out her spoon. "I love walnuts."

Alex pushed her spoon away. Fishing several walnuts out of his sundae with his own spoon, he held it out across the table. "Here you go, Lisa. Sweets for my sweetie."

"Gag me." Stevie rolled her eyes as Alex fed Lisa the walnuts.

Alex wiggled his eyebrows at her in mock menace. "That can be arranged, sister dear."

"Mmm. That marshmallow is good." Lisa licked her lips, then smiled at her boyfriend beseechingly. "How about another bite?"

Alex scooped up a spoonful of marshmallow topping. "Anything for you."

Stevie rolled her eyes again. "I think this is my cue to leave," she announced, shoving at Alex so that he'd let her out of the booth. "If I have to watch you two lovebirds feeding each other much longer, I may never eat again." Stevie really was ready to leave. The mood at their table was weirding her out, and besides, she still hadn't come any closer to figuring out what to do about Scott. Callie, though sympathetic, hadn't been much help. And Alex and Lisa were even less likely to have anything useful to contribute, especially since they were clearly slipping fast into their most annoying, goofily romantic mood. She glanced at Callie. "Want a lift home?"

"Hi, it's me," Stevie said into the phone a few minutes later. She had just arrived home after dropping Callie off. Nobody else was around, so Stevie was lying on the couch in the living room with the phone on her stomach. "What's up?"

"Hey, Stevie," Phil replied from the other end of the line. "Not much. I just got in."

"Really?" Stevie glanced at her watch. It was almost dinnertime. "Did you go riding today?"

"Not yet. I was just getting ready to go out and check on Teddy." Phil's family had a small stable on their property, where Phil kept his horse. "Actually, I was with your buddy Scott."

Stevie wasn't sure she had heard him right. "Scott Forester?"

"No, Scott of the Antarctic," Phil said. He chuckled. "Yeah, I mean Scott Forester. He invited me over to shoot some hoops again."

"How nice." Stevie grimaced, glad that Phil couldn't see her.

"He's a really cool guy, you know, Stevie," Phil went on. "I mean, I know you two have some problems, but I think if you just gave each other a chance, started out fresh—"

"Why are you telling me this?" Stevie snapped, annoyed at his tone. "I'm not the one playing silent treatment here, you know. You ought to save your breath for telling your good friend Scott how cool *I* am instead of the other way around."

"I didn't mean it that way," Phil protested. "I

mean, it's just that I like Scott a lot. And of course you know I'm crazy about you. I really want you two to make up so that we can all be friends."

Stevie gripped the phone more tightly. Phil was usually a bright guy, which made it all the harder to believe how dense he was being. "Look, save your pep talk," she said irritably. "I don't need to hear it. In case you didn't notice, Scott's the one to blame for us not being pals. Not me."

"I know, I know," Phil said. "But—"

Stevie interrupted. "Listen, I've gotta go," she said. "Talk to you later." She slammed the phone down. At times like these, guys were more trouble than they were worth.

FOURTEEN

By the time the final bell rang the following day, Stevie was starting to feel a little guilty about hanging up on Phil. He had called her back after dinner, but she'd had Alex tell him she was in the shower. Now she realized that maybe she had been a little hard on Phil. He was only trying to help.

With trying *being the operative word*, she thought as she dumped her books in her locker and headed for the exit. Sitting through yet another chemistry lab from hell had only reinforced her opinion that Phil had been way off base. Scott had spent the entire class period that day teasing Sue about her daisy-shaped barrettes and totally ignoring Stevie. It was getting harder to take with every passing day, and the only thing that had kept Stevie from asking to be moved to a different group was the fact that they'd had a substitute teacher.

She blinked as she stepped out of the school building into the bright afternoon sunlight. As she walked down the crumbling stone steps toward the student parking lot, she saw someone waving at her. Her eyes widened in surprise.

"Phil?" she whispered. Her heart soared. She couldn't believe he was there.

She sped up, taking the steps two at a time. Soon she was close enough to leap at him and give him a kiss.

He kissed her back, laughing at the same time. "Hi, Stevie!" he said as she pulled away. "Nice to see you, too."

"Well?" she said, smiling and waiting.

"Well what?"

Her smile wavered. "You know," she said impatiently, punching him lightly on the arm. "Aren't you going to tell me why you're here?"

"Oh!" Phil shrugged. "Right. I told Scott I'd pick him up. We're supposed to hit the country club for a few games of tennis, and his car's being inspected."

Stevie felt her face go hot while her insides turned to ice. "You're here to see . . . Scott?" she said evenly.

Phil seemed to recognize that something was wrong. He gave her that weird, conciliatory half smile he always used when he thought she might be mad at him but wasn't sure why. "Yeah, I was going to tell you about it on the phone yesterday, but you hung up before I got the chance. What was that all about, anyway?"

Stevie was clenching her fists so hard her fingers were starting to go numb. She couldn't believe Phil could be so totally, completely, irredeemably clueless. She felt uncontrollable rage bubbling up inside her. Scott Forester had been making her life miserable for too long, and now he had enlisted her boyfriend to make things even worse. First they had spoiled Pine Hollow by hanging out together there, making it even more uncomfortable for her at the stable than it had been before. Now they were meeting at her school. What next? Would her parents invite the two of them to dinner so that she could be humiliated in her own home, too?

"I'll tell you what this is about," Stevie cried, taking a step closer and poking Phil sharply in the chest. "This is about your bad—no, make that your horrible, excruciatingly horrible—taste in new friends. I mean, you know how Scott treats me. You've seen it with your own eyes."

Phil raised his hands in front of him in a gesture of appeasement. "I know. But listen, Stevie—"

"No, you listen." Stevie was really getting warmed up now. She had held this in for too long. She was sick of being the mature one about it. "Scott Forester pretends to be this great, nice, likable, friendly guy. But he's not. He's a—a jerk. He treats me like dirt, and for what? Because he thinks I'm to blame for hurting his sister. Well, guess what?" Stevie spread her arms wide, her voice rising. "Guess what? His sister doesn't blame me. Nobody blames me except him. So where does he get off? Does he think he's so damn important, so high and mighty, that he's allowed to judge me like that? Is he so perfect that he never made a mistake? Or so stupid he doesn't know the meaning of the word *accident*? Has it occurred to him that my driving might have saved his sister's life? Maybe he's just mad that Callie's problems aren't something he can argue away in his precious debate club! Poor baby. Maybe he just needs to grow up and get over it."

Stevie noticed that Phil's face was turning redder and redder by the second. *Good*, she thought with satisfaction. *Maybe that means he's finally getting it.*

Then another thought occurred to her. She gulped. She turned around slowly. Scott Forester was standing a few feet behind her.

Stevie froze. Her mind went blank, refusing to accept the truth—that Scott must have heard all the horrible things she had shouted about him. Shouted for the entire parking lot full of students to hear.

"Well, Stevie," Scott said evenly after a terrible moment of silence. "I guess now we know who *won't* be voted most tactful in the Fenton Hall yearbook this year."

It was the longest sentence he'd addressed to her in months, and it jolted her out of her momentary confusion. Her hands on her hips, she glared at him, ignoring Phil, who was making ineffectual soothing noises behind her. "Listen," she said. "I've reached the limit with you. You've been doing your best to make me miserable for a long time now, and I'm sick of it." She waved one hand wildly in the air to punctuate her point. "But that isn't enough for you, is it, Mr. Vindictive? Now you're trying to make me flunk chemistry, too. Well, congratulations. I guess that means I'll see you in summer school next year. Maybe we can even be lab partners again. Won't *that* be fun?"

Scott's angry expression settled into a stubborn look. "I don't know what you're talking about," he said loudly. "Don't blame me if you can't handle your classes."

"Oh, please!" Stevie exclaimed, laughing sharply in pure disbelief. She shook off Phil's hand, which was tugging desperately on her arm. Could Scott really be this dense? Had his grudge totally warped his mind? "Now you're trying to pin that on me, too? Unbelievable."

"Give me a break. You—" Scott began hotly.

Stevie cut him off to correct herself, drowning out his words by the sheer force and volume of her own. "Actually, maybe it's not so unbelievable.

You've been blaming me for just about everything lately short of the weather, but I'm sure that if you thought it was too hot or too wet or too whatever, that would be my fault, too!"

"You don't know what you're talking about," Scott said through clenched teeth. "I don't have to stand here and listen to this garbage." He spun on his heel and started to walk away.

But Stevie wasn't finished with him yet. She leaped forward and grabbed his shoulder, forcing him to turn and face her. Phil hurried after her, once again murmuring something about calming down. But Stevie didn't feel like calming down. "Yes, you do have to listen," she shouted into Scott's scowling face, dropping her hands to her sides. "You do have to listen to me. Because I can't take this anymore—this idiotic grudge of yours, I mean. It's gone on long enough. It's stupid and petty and immature, and in case you didn't notice, it isn't doing one single thing to help Callie get better. If anything, it's probably making things harder for her."

Scott glared at her for a moment. Stevie glared back, her fists clenched at her sides, ignoring the curious glances of passing students. Scott had started this, and she wasn't about to back down. If he wanted a fight, she would give it to him. In fact, she welcomed it. Anything would be better than continuing as they had been.

Then, to her total amazement, Scott's face crumpled. His mouth, which had been held in a straight, taut line, quivered. His narrowed eyes grew watery. A tear escaped and trickled down his cheek. A moment later, he buried his face in his hands and started to cry.

That was the last thing Stevie had expected. Startled, she glanced at Phil for help. Phil looked as surprised as she did, but he reacted quickly. Grabbing Stevie's arm with one hand and Scott's with the other, he dragged them off behind a minivan, away from the prying eyes of their fellow students.

Scott leaned back against the metal side of the van, his arm flung across his face. Stevie just stared at him, still speechless. Phil stood quietly nearby, his face averted, apparently content now to wait it out.

After a moment, Scott gave one last shuddering sigh and lowered his arm. He didn't meet Stevie's eye as he wiped his face with the hem of his shirt. "Sorry about that," he murmured, his voice so low that it was barely audible. "I mean—sorry."

Stevie wasn't sure what to say. "Are you okay?" she ventured cautiously after a moment.

Now Scott raised his eyes to hers. "No," he answered. "I guess I'm not okay. I thought I was. But it's pretty obvious now that I'm not."

Phil spoke for the first time. "Hey, man," he said to Scott in that gruff voice that guys always seemed to use in any kind of personal discussion with other guys. "You don't have to explain."

"Yes he does!" Stevie said quickly, feeling her indignation rise again. She shot her boyfriend an irritated look. Just because big, tough, manly Scott Forester had shed a few tears didn't mean she was letting him off the hook. The show of emotion might have confused Phil, but it had only made her more eager to hash this out once and for all. She turned back to Scott and crossed her arms over her chest. "Listen," she said. She wasn't shouting anymore, but she kept her voice firm. "What's going on here, anyway?"

Scott shrugged and ran one hand through his thick, wavy hair. "I don't know."

Stevie frowned slightly. It still felt strange to have Scott responding to her after so long, but so far he wasn't shedding much light on anything.

"Just answer me one question, okay?" Stevie waited for Scott to nod before continuing. "Why have you been torturing me all this time?"

"I don't know," Scott said again, heavily. "I don't know."

That wasn't good enough for Stevie. Not now. Not when they had come this far. "Come on, you can do better than that," she said bluntly. "What did I ever to do you—I mean really? It can't just be about the accident. Can it?"

For a moment she didn't think Scott was going to answer. She heard Phil shifting his feet uneasily at her side, but she didn't take her eyes off Scott as a range of emotions—anger, sadness, pride, and something else, perhaps fear?—played across his handsome face.

Finally he heaved a long, deep sigh and blinked quickly a few times. "I haven't really been asking myself that," he said slowly, breaking away from Stevie's intense gaze and staring at the blacktop. "I should have, I think." He swallowed hard. When he continued, his voice sounded steadier. "I know I should have. You're right to be angry, Stevie. I guess maybe I haven't been fair."

Stevie opened her mouth to agree, but Phil shot her a look and shook his head. Realizing he was right, she clamped her mouth shut again and waited for Scott to go on.

"I know everyone thinks of me as this easygoing, relaxed kind of guy," Scott said, tapping his fingers nervously on the van. "I sort of like having them think that. But it's not really the truth. I worry about a lot of stuff. I—I just don't like to let people see that. I'm not sure why."

Stevie had a pretty good guess about that. It was obvious to anyone who had seen them together that

Scott modeled much of his personality and behavior on his father. As a politician hungry for public approval—which translated into votes—Congressman Forester couldn't afford to let his guard down, to appear weak or vulnerable or uncertain, or angry or upset. Even after Callie's accident, the congressman had told reporters merely that he was optimistic about her recovery. That didn't give Scott much to go on. But Stevie decided to keep her theory to herself, for the moment at least.

"So why break the mold for me?" Stevie asked. "I mean, you haven't exactly been easygoing and relaxed when I've been around lately. Anybody could see that."

"I know. I think that's part of the reason I've stayed so angry." Scott shrugged. "I guess I blamed you for that, too—for making me look like a jerk in front of other people."

Phil cleared his throat. "Stevie wasn't the one who made you look like a jerk, Scott," he said.

Scott nodded. "I know, I know." He sighed and shook his head. "I don't know what I was thinking all this time. I guess I *wasn't* thinking, or at least I wasn't thinking straight."

Stevie was getting a little impatient with all this introspection. She was glad that Scott was getting to know himself better, but where did that leave her? "You still didn't answer my question," she said.

"Why were you so mad at me in the first place? I mean, I could sort of understand it at the beginning. You were worried about your sister, and you didn't know me that well—I probably would have jumped to some conclusions, too. But then Callie forgave me, and the police . . ." She let her words trail away. She had been over this so many times before; in her own head, with her friends and family and other people. Even the thought of it made her weary.

Scott shrugged and, for a second, seemed unwilling to answer. Then he spoke up again, still sounding reluctant. "I don't know," he said. "I really don't."

"Listen, Scott," Phil said. "This isn't really my business. But if you want to know what I think, I think it's because you're kind of a control freak."

Duh! Stevie thought. She could have told both guys that ages ago. It was obvious in everything Scott did, from debate club to driving his sister to all her therapeutic riding sessions.

Scott shot Phil a quick, angry glance. But then he seemed to stop and think about what he'd said. "What do you mean by that?" he asked quietly.

Phil looked a bit uncomfortable, but he went on. "It's like the other day at the country club," he said. "You got all upset just because someone else ran past us and got the court we wanted."

"Come on!" Scott said quickly. "You saw that jerk. He was totally out of line. I mean, I couldn't—Oh." He wrinkled his brow. There was a long pause before he spoke again. "I guess I see what you mean."

"That could be why Callie's accident hit you so hard," Phil continued. "I mean, nobody could have prevented it. Nobody could have predicted it. It just happened—out of anyone's control." He snapped his fingers to illustrate. "Out of *your* control." He glanced at Stevie somberly. "That's why it was so important for you to find someone to blame."

At first Stevie didn't get it. Then she nodded as understanding dawned. What Phil was saying was foreign to her in one way, since she herself had never feared the unknown—in theory, at least. Part of what she loved about life was its unpredictable nature. She welcomed that, embraced it, thrived on it. But once, when Alex had been gravely ill with meningitis, she had realized how hard it could be not to know the answers to certain questions when someone you loved was involved.

"I get it," she said, staring at Scott as she worked through it in her own mind. "You pinned it all on me. If you convinced yourself that I was totally responsible for what happened to Callie, you wouldn't have to think about the bigger picture. The fact that accidents happen and people get hurt, even die. You didn't really want to think about that possibility, did you? You just needed someone to be responsible."

"Well," Scott said. He looked even more uncomfortable than Phil did. "I guess you two have me all figured out, huh?" But his words didn't sound hostile. In fact, his voice was weary and sad.

Stevie exchanged glances with Phil. She had no idea what to say next, and she could tell he didn't, either. "Listen, Scott—" she began tentatively.

He held up a hand to silence her, not meeting her eye. "No, let me say something," he said in that same weary tone. "I'm sorry about all this. Me and you, I mean. It's all my fault. It was wrong, really unfair. I'm sorry. I don't blame you if you hate me right now." He lifted his head and looked her square in the face. "But I hope—I mean, can you— Can we start over again? Try to be friends, or at least not enemies?"

Stevie rubbed her face and sighed. She wasn't sure what she was feeling. This whole conversation had been one big surprise from beginning to end. And Scott had put her through so much misery for so long . . . But what was the point of dwelling on that? Stevie had never been one to wallow in self-pity. It was time to move on.

"Sure," she told Scott, managing a slight smile. "I'd like that."

Scott looked relieved. "Good," he said. He returned her smile. "Maybe this way we can both even manage to pass chem this semester."

Stevie grimaced. "Let's not get crazy here," she joked.

Phil stepped forward. He seemed relieved, too. "This has been fun," he said, keeping his voice light and casual. "But why don't we get out of here? Maybe the three of us could grab a bite to eat somewhere."

"That's a great idea." Scott glanced at Phil gratefully, then turned back to Stevie. "But I have an even better one. Phil and I were going to play some tennis this afternoon. Why don't you come along to the club with us? We could all hit a few balls around . . . you know. Not exactly mixed doubles, but it could be fun."

Stevie hesitated. "Thanks. But I don't think so." She would be ready to start patching up her relationship with Scott soon. But for today, she thought she would rather just go home and think about all this. "You two go ahead, though. I'll catch you both later."

Phil peered into her eyes, looking concerned. "Really?" he asked uncertainly. "Are you sure you're okay?"

"Really. I'm sure." And this time, she meant it.

———

By the time she walked into chemistry class three days later, it felt almost natural for Stevie to greet Scott with a friendly smile and a little wave as she took her seat next to him at lab table number four. Sue was absent, so it was just the two of them.

"Hi, Stevie," Scott greeted her as he dropped his lab notebook onto the black tabletop. "What's new?"

"Not much." Stevie still felt kind of weird chatting with Scott this way—as if nothing had happened, as if the past three months had merely been an extended bad dream. But she was trying to ignore those feelings, and it was getting easier with every passing day. "You?"

Scott shrugged. "Callie had another doctor's appointment today," he reported. "At lunchtime. Sounds like it went pretty well."

"Great!" Stevie said. "I haven't seen her all day. But she must be thrilled, especially after last time."

Scott turned away long enough to greet several female classmates who had stopped to say hi, giggling and batting their eyelashes. Stevie rolled her eyes. But Scott's charm and charisma didn't really bother her anymore. For one thing, because she was no longer angry at him, they no longer seemed like a personal affront. But also, she now knew how much that seemingly effortless charm cost him.

That made her feel a lot more sympathetic toward him.

When the girls had moved on to their own tables, Scott returned his attention to Stevie. "What did you say about Callie's last appointment?"

Stevie shrugged. "I talked to her afterward," she said. "She seemed pretty disappointed by what the doctor told her. I guess she was hoping for better news about losing the crutches. But the doc said she was stuck with them until November at least."

"Hmmm." Scott was silent for a moment.

Stevie watched him curiously. She wasn't shy, and according to her mother and Lisa and various other people, she wasn't always tactful. But she hesitated to ask Scott what he was thinking. Their relationship was still too new, untested and a little uncertain.

Luckily, Scott decided to volunteer the information. "It's interesting to hear that," he said. "Because actually, that was good news. Before, Dr. Amandsen was predicting Callie would be able to walk without any assistance sometime after Christmas, maybe not until the very early spring. But thanks to all her hard work, he moved that up a couple of months. We were all thrilled." He glanced at Stevie. "All except Callie, apparently."

Stevie bit her lip, wondering if she had given

away some kind of secret without realizing it. "She didn't seem that upset," she said quickly. "I mean, I was kind of rushed that day I think, so maybe I—"

"It's okay," Scott reassured her. "It's not so surprising to hear that she reacted that way. I know why she's so eager to ditch the crutches right now. It's because her friend Sheila is coming to visit next week. Did she tell you about that?"

Stevie nodded, wondering why Scott's lip had curled slightly as he said Sheila's name. "She didn't say she was coming so soon, but she mentioned it a couple of times," she said. "She seemed pretty psyched about it. Don't you like Sheila?"

Scott looked surprised for a moment. Then he laughed. "Is it that obvious?" he asked. "Uh-oh. I'd better work on that before she gets here."

Stevie grinned. "You're secret's safe with me," she promised. "Don't worry—I don't always like my brothers' friends that much, either."

"Well, I guess that's only natural." Scott glanced at the front of the classroom as Ms. Rourke entered. When the teacher started talking quietly with a student who'd been waiting by her desk, Scott went on. "But there's a little more to it than that when it comes to Callie and Sheila."

"What do you mean?"

Scott sighed. "I know it's probably none of my

business," he said. "Callie's a big girl—she can pick her own friends. But Sheila . . . well, in my opinion Sheila has never been that good for her. She and Callie have always been close—our mothers are good friends—but not in the same way you and your friends are close."

Stevie wasn't following him. "Huh?"

Scott looked pensive. "You and your friends share things, support each other. Right?" When Stevie nodded, he went on. "Callie and Sheila aren't really that way. They always seem to think— at least Callie does—that they have to put on some kind of front for each other, be perfect friends, perfect people."

That didn't make any sense at all to Stevie, and she said so.

"I know. It's weird," Scott agreed. "But that's how it's always been with those two. Sort of competitive, in a warped way. Like they're one step removed from what most people think of as friendship, each of them doing their best to prove to the other what a wonderful friend she is."

"Wow." Stevie was still having trouble wrapping her mind around that, though it did help to explain Callie's rather odd behavior at TD's when she was telling Lisa about Sheila. Still, it was so different from most of the friendships Stevie knew—her friendship with Carole and Lisa, Phil's friendship with A.J.—that it was hard to imagine.

"I'm sure my family's lifestyle is partly to blame," Scott said thoughtfully. "It's not easy living in a fishbowl like we do, with people always watching because of Dad's job. Sometimes it's hard to know who to trust."

"You don't seem to have much trouble," Stevie pointed out. Remembering what she now knew about him, she added, "Most of the time, anyway."

"I don't," Scott admitted with a shrug. "I like people, and it's always been pretty easy for me to make friends. But Callie's different. She's always been kind of withdrawn, serious, maybe a little suspicious. It's harder for her to let her guard down. That's probably why she got so interested in horses so young. She's always trusted them a lot more than people, I think."

"Makes sense to me," Stevie joked. Then she frowned. "So why is Sheila coming to visit, then?"

Scott shrugged again. "Because despite all that, Callie thinks of her as her best friend. Besides, this move has been pretty tough on her. She hides it most of the time, but I'm pretty sure she still thinks a lot about our old home. Sheila is part of that, so of course she wants to see her."

Suddenly something clicked for Stevie. "But at the same time, she doesn't want Sheila to see her with her weak leg and the rest of it, because it proves she's not perfect after all. That's why she wanted to be able to get rid of her crutches. She wanted to be all better before Sheila gets here."

"Bingo." Scott smiled, but his eyes were sad. "Callie hates looking weak in front of anyone. But she must really hate the thought of Sheila seeing her the way she is now."

Stevie frowned. "Well, I think that's terrible," she declared. "Friends should trust each other. They should accept each other as they are, weaknesses and all."

"I know." Scott sighed. "I just wish Callie saw that as clearly as you do."

At that moment the teacher called for attention, bringing their conversation to an end. But Stevie continued to think about what Scott had just told her. She thought it was truly sad that Callie couldn't simply be happy about a visit from her oldest friend. *Maybe I can help her,* Stevie thought hopefully. *Maybe I can find a chance to talk with her about this before Sheila gets here next week. If Sheila is a true friend, Callie just needs to learn to trust her. They need to start trusting each other, being honest with each other—warts and all. If I can help her see that, this visit could be the start of a whole new Callie.*

Stevie smiled, pleased with her new plan. She

would help Callie feel better about her friend's visit, and in the process show her what real friendship was all about. It sounded like a big job, but Stevie was sure she could do it.

Now that Scott and I are talking again, she told herself happily, *just about anything seems possible!*

FIFTEEN

"Well, here we go again," Stevie said, clicking the Power button on the remote control. "Another thrilling Friday night in front of the TV."

Phil put his arm around her and pulled her a little closer on the couch. "You can't fool me," he teased, nuzzling her neck. "This is your favorite way to spend Friday night."

Lisa glanced over her shoulder at them from her spot in the overstuffed chair. "Little do you know," she told Phil mischievously. "Actually Stevie's favorite part about all this is watching all those hot hunks on Skye's show." She gestured at the television, where the opening credits for *Paradise Ranch* were coming onto the screen.

"Shhh!" Stevie pretended to be worried. "You'll give my secret away!"

Lisa giggled, then settled back in her chair with a glance at the archway leading to the Lakes' kitchen. "Hurry up, Alex," she called. "It's starting."

Alex appeared in the archway with a couple of soda cans in each hand. "I'm coming, I'm coming," he said. "Make room."

As he set the drinks down on the coffee table, Lisa stood and waited for him to sit down before settling herself comfortably on his lap. Leaning over to grab her soda, she looked at the screen just as Skye Ransom's name flashed across it, accompanied by a shot of the young actor's smiling, handsome face. She still felt a bit strange about watching the show with Alex, even though they had seen it together almost every Friday night since its premiere at the end of August.

Don't look for trouble, she told herself sternly, popping the top on her soda and feeling Alex's strong arm squeeze her waist as she settled back against his chest. *Alex seems to be getting over his jealousy about Skye. And that means maybe someday soon I'll be able to talk to him about the other stuff. About almost staying in California. I just want to wait until I'm sure he'll understand.*

She did her best to forget the whole subject and concentrate on the show. But she found herself having trouble following the plot, even though she had been on the set when the episode had been filmed.

Finally the first commercial break came. Stevie stretched and scooted away from Phil a few inches. "All this soda is very well and good," she said. "But what does a girl have to do to get some popcorn around here?"

Phil jumped to his feet and saluted. "Aye, aye, ma'am!" he said with a mock salute. He gestured to Alex. "Come on, dude. We're on kitchen duty."

Stevie giggled and winked at Lisa. "He's so well trained," she confided in a loud whisper.

Lisa giggled, too. Alex rolled his eyes and then stood, pushing her aside gently. "Normally I'd be the last person to do something just because Stevie ordered it," he said. "But in this case, popcorn does sound pretty good. And if we want to be able to eat it, Phil and I had better make it, because Stevie's the only person I know who can actually burn a whole bag of microwave popcorn."

A moment later both guys had disappeared into the kitchen. Stevie smiled as she heard the faint sounds of the two of them talking and laughing together. This was nice. Being here, with her favorite people in the world . . . well, most of them, anyway.

"Hey, by the way, why couldn't Carole make it tonight?" she asked Lisa. "You never said."

Lisa shrugged as she dug her lip balm out of her jeans pocket and ran it over her lips. "She didn't really say," she said, popping the cap back on. "I just saw her in the hall for a second before last period. When I reminded her it was *Paradise Ranch* night, she got that look on her face. You know the one."

"The one that means she totally forgot." Stevie nodded and smiled ruefully. "Good old Carole." She sighed. "Sometimes I hate going to a different school than you guys. I feel like I've hardly seen Carole at all this past month."

"I don't know if you can blame separate schools for that," Lisa said. "I haven't been seeing a whole lot of her myself. I know she always spends most of her time at Pine Hollow. . . ."

"But these days it seems like she's spending *all* her time there. Oh, well, at least we'll see her tomorrow—unless she gets so busy cleaning Starlight's hooves or braiding Samson's mane that she forgets about our movie plans, too." Stevie tucked her legs up under her on the sofa and looked at Lisa thoughtfully. "I guess we all have a lot on our plates these days, don't we?"

Lisa was a little surprised at Stevie's serious tone. But she suspected she knew what her friend was thinking. "How are things going between you and Scott?"

Stevie shrugged. "So far, so good," she said. "I mean, it's only been a few days. But he's trying. And so am I."

"Good." Lisa was really happy that Stevie had finally made up with Callie's brother. She wasn't sure exactly what had happened to finally break down Scott's grudge—Stevie had been rather mysterious about that, and Lisa hadn't pressed her—but it was wonderful to see the difference the change had already wrought in her. Now, when Scott approached her in the aisle at Pine Hollow, Stevie's face no longer took on that slightly wary, haunted expression. Now the two of them greeted each other politely, chatted easily about Callie's progress or horses or chemistry homework. Maybe they still weren't bosom buddies, not yet, but it was a start. A good start. *Now if I can just learn to be friends with Callie . . .* Lisa picked at the arm of her chair. "Scott's a nice guy," she mused, wishing that a little of his friendliness would rub off on his sister. Maybe that would make this easier. . . .

Stevie noticed that Lisa's voice sounded funny. She glanced at her, noting the pensive look on her fine-boned face as she stared down into her lap.

"Is anything wrong?" Stevie asked. "You sound kind of weird."

Lisa looked up and smiled ruefully. "Sorry," she said softly, glancing toward the kitchen to make sure the boys weren't returning yet. "It's nothing major. Just some stupid stuff that I have to work out in my own head, I guess."

"Tell me," Stevie ordered, leaning forward.

Lisa shrugged. "It's . . . Well, it's Callie," she

admitted softly. "I haven't said anything up until now because—well, I don't know. I guess it hasn't really come up. But things feel a little weird between me and Callie."

Stevie was surprised for a second. Then she remembered that awkward day at TD's and nodded. "I guess that's not a total shock," she said. "I mean, I know you don't know her as well as Carole and I do. But I thought you two hit it off pretty well when she moved here."

"Right," Lisa said, reaching for her soda. "But then I went away, and when I came back, you and Carole and Callie were like best buddies all of a sudden." She couldn't help allowing a touch of bitterness to creep into her voice.

"It wasn't all of a sudden," Stevie reminded her bluntly. "You were gone a long time. Carole and I had plenty of time to get to know Callie better. Especially since she was spending a lot of time at Pine Hollow working on her physical therapy."

That made Lisa feel more than a little guilty. Poor Callie. First she had moved far away from her home and her friends; then she had suffered that terrible accident, along with months of recovery that still hadn't ended. Lisa didn't envy her that. She just wished she knew how to work the idea of Callie into her own view of life, of her relationship with her best friends.

"I know," Lisa told Stevie with a sigh. "I have some catching up to do. And I'm sure Callie and I will be good friends before long." She wasn't quite as certain as her optimistic words proclaimed. But she had learned enough from her mother's example lately to know that bitterness and gloom and refusing to accept things as they were didn't solve anything. They just made people even more miserable.

Luckily, Stevie changed the subject. "Speaking of Callie and friends, Scott told me something kind of juicy in lab today."

"Give." Lisa glanced toward the kitchen again. They could hear popcorn popping. "And hurry. The show's starting again, and the guys'll be back any second."

Stevie glanced at the television, where Skye was gazing soulfully into the eyes of a beautiful actress. "Hey, maybe we should pipe down and watch," she teased.

Lisa glared at her. "Stevie . . ."

Stevie shrugged and feigned innocence. "I mean, we wouldn't want to miss a second of this show you slaved on all summer just for a little news, would we?"

Lisa jumped out of her chair and grabbed Stevie by the arm. "Tell me," she commanded. "Or I'll wrestle you to the ground and then steal all the popcorn."

Stevie giggled and jerked her arm away. "You and what army?" But at Lisa's threatening growl, she held up both hands. "Okay, okay. You win."

Lisa settled herself back on the couch next to Stevie. "Let's hear it."

"Well, our other lab partner was absent today. So Scott and I got to talking." Stevie paused for a second, thinking about that. Up until three days ago, she had dreaded the very thought of walking into chemistry class each day, because she knew she would have to deal with silent Scott. *Now I just dread it because I hate chemistry,* she joked to herself. Realizing that Lisa was waiting impatiently for her to go on, she did so, relaying what Scott had told her about Callie and Sheila.

"Weird," was Lisa's only comment when she had finished. The two of them fell silent for a moment, thinking their own thoughts as they watched the action on the TV screen.

"Anyway," Stevie said after a moment, "I'm going to try to help her if I can."

Lisa nodded. She could have predicted that. Stevie was a good friend—to all her friends. New ones like Callie as well as older ones . . . That line of thought reminded Lisa of something else. "Hey," she said. "I forgot to ask. Is anything new with A.J.?"

Stevie made a face and shook her head. "Not as

far as I can tell," she said with a sigh. "I still haven't set eyes on him since the breakup, but Phil's awfully low about it all. Something's got to give soon, I think. Otherwise we'll all go crazy."

Lisa smiled sympathetically and leaned over to get her soda. "I'm sure it'll all work out," she said. "A.J.'s cool. Everything will be all right." At that moment, a character on the TV show rode onscreen on a tall bay horse—a horse that looked enough like Prancer to start Lisa's mind off in another direction. She hesitated, not sure how to ask Stevie what she wanted to ask.

Before she could figure it out, the two guys burst back into the room, laughing loudly at some private joke. Alex was carrying a big bowl of popcorn in the crook of one arm and a pile of napkins in his hand. Phil had brought more sodas.

"Here we are," Phil said, plopping down on the couch next to Stevie.

Alex wedged himself into the remaining space beside Lisa and slung his arm around her, accidentally brushing his hand against Stevie's ear as he did.

"Hey!" Stevie said indignantly. "Watch it, you big clumsy doofus."

Alex leaned over and smacked Stevie lightly on the side of the head. "Oops," he said with a grin. "Sorry."

"Enough!" Lisa shoved Alex aside so that he

couldn't reach Stevie anymore. "Can't you see we're trying to concentrate on the show?"

Alex rolled his eyes elaborately. "Sor-ry," he drawled. "Is that the thanks we get for slaving over a hot microwave to bring you this popcorn?"

Lisa smiled and gave him a quick kiss. "Nope," she said, leaning forward to grab a handful of warm popcorn. "*That's* the thanks you get."

"And this is the thanks you get from me," Stevie added, leaning across Lisa to smack Alex soundly on the leg.

Alex, Stevie, and Phil continued to joke around and jostle each other for a moment. Then they all settled down and turned their attention back to *Paradise Ranch.* But Lisa found her mind wandering to other things, since, thanks to her job on the set, she already knew how the story turned out.

Too bad life isn't more like TV, she mused. *On TV everything always gets wrapped up in half an hour or an hour. If life were like that, maybe we wouldn't all have to spend so much time wondering and worrying about what's going to happen next. Like Stevie wasting all those months trying to figure out what would happen with Scott, or Carole worrying about whether Ben is still mad at her for following him home, or Alex getting all upset about me spending time with Skye this summer.* She bit her lip and glanced again at the bay horse loping across the imaginary ranch on the

230

screen. *And then there's the situation with Prancer. I really wish I knew how that was going to turn out, what Max is being so secretive about. It may be something totally innocent, like that Max is buying Judy out. On the other hand . . .*

She didn't like to think too much about the other hand. She just wished she'd had time to mention her worries to Stevie before the guys had come back. She knew it was silly—there couldn't be anything seriously wrong with Prancer, it just wasn't possible—but she would feel better if she talked it over with Stevie, got her opinion on the whole thing. Maybe she could find an opportunity to bring it up later.

Stevie's mind was drifting along different lines. As she snuggled against Phil, half her attention on the television, she was still thinking about Scott. *It's amazing what a difference a few days can make,* she thought idly. *A week ago, I would have thought there was no chance for me and Scott to ever be friends. And now here we are, practically best buddies.*

She realized she was exaggerating a little. But she couldn't help it. Now that she and Scott had made up at last, it made her feel a lot more optimistic about some of the other things that had been going on lately. If she and Scott could put their differences behind them, almost anything could happen. A.J. could come to his senses and act normal again. Lisa and Callie could make up for lost time and be pals. Callie could arrive at a new understanding with her friend from back home. Carole could wake up and realize that she and Ben had a major crush on each other—and maybe even realize that there might be more to life than horses. A little more, anyway.

Okay, so maybe that last one's kind of a long shot, Stevie thought, smiling to herself as she leaned forward to grab a handful of popcorn. *I mean, Carole couldn't even drag herself away from Pine Hollow long enough to spend a lazy Friday night in front of the TV. But the rest of it could happen, just like that, without any warning at all. You just never know what's coming. And I guess that's just one of the things that makes life a lot cooler than TV!*

ABOUT THE AUTHOR

BONNIE BRYANT is the author of more than a hundred books about horses, including The Saddle Club series, Saddle Club Super Editions, and the Pony Tails series. She has also written novels and movie novelizations under her married name, B. B. Hiller.

Ms. Bryant began writing The Saddle Club in 1986. Although she had done some riding before that, she intensified her studies then and found herself learning right along with her characters Stevie, Carole, and Lisa. She claims that they are all much better riders than she is.

Ms. Bryant was born and raised in New York City. She still lives there, in Greenwich Village, with her two sons.